A WINDOW IN THRUMS

AN EDINBURGH ELEVEN

No. 1809

THE SQUARE FOOT OF GLASS WHERE JESS SAT IN HER CHAIR
AND LOOKED DOWN THE BRAE

A WINDOW IN THRUMS

AN EDINBURGH ELEVEN

BY

J. M. BARRIE

NEW YORK

CHARLES SCRIBNER'S SONS

1921

823.91   B275w

1809

THE SCRIBNER PRESS

INTRODUCTION*

WHEN the English publishers read "A Window in Thrums" in manuscript they thought it unbearably sad and begged me to alter the end. They warned me that the public do not like sad books. Well, the older I grow and the sadder the things I see, the more do I wish my books to be bright and hopeful, but an author may not always interfere with his story, and if I had altered the end of "A Window in Thrums" I think I should never have had any more respect for myself. It is a sadder book to me than it can ever be to anyone else. I see Jess at her window looking for the son who never came back as no other can see her, and I knew that unless I brought him back in time the book would be a pain to me all my days, but the thing had to be done.

I think there are soft-hearted readers here and there who will be glad to know that there never was any Jess. There is a little house still standing at the top of the brae which can be identified as her house, I chose it for her though I was never in it myself, but it is only the places in my books about Thrums that may be identified. The men and women, with indeed some very subsidiary exceptions, who now and again cross the square, are entirely imaginary, and Jess is of them. But anything in her that was rare or beautiful she had from my mother; the imaginary woman came to me as I looked into the eyes of the real one. And as it is the love of mother and son that has written everything of mine that is of any worth, it was natural that the awful horror of the untrue son should dog my thoughts and call upon me to paint the picture. That, I believe now, though I had no idea of it at the time, is how " A Window in Thrums " came to be written, less by me than by an impulse from behind. And so it wrote itself, very quickly. I have read that I rewrote it eight times, but it was written once only, nearly every chapter, I think, at a sitting.

A WINDOW IN THRUMS

CONTENTS

AN EDINBURGH ELEVEN

A WINDOW IN THRUMS

A WINDOW IN THRUMS

CHAPTER I

THE HOUSE ON THE BRAE

ON the bump of green round which the brae twists, at the top of the brae, and within cry of T'nowhead Farm, still stands a one-storey house, whose whitewashed walls, streaked with the discoloration that rain leaves, look yellow when the snow comes. In the old days the stiff ascent left Thrums behind, and where is now the making of a suburb was only a poor row of dwellings and a manse, with Hendry's cot to watch the brae. The house stood bare, without a shrub, in a garden whose paling did not go all the way round, the potato pit being only kept out of the road, that here sets off southward, by a broken dyke of stones and earth. On each side of the slate-coloured door was a window of knotted glass. Ropes were flung over the thatch to keep the roof on in wind.

Into this humble abode I would take any one

who cares to accompany me. But you must not come in a contemptuous mood, thinking that the poor are but a stage removed from beasts of burden, as some cruel writers of these days say; nor will I have you turn over with your foot the shabby horse-hair chairs that Leeby kept so speckless, and Hendry weaved for years to buy, and Jess so loved to look upon.

I speak of the chairs, but if we go together into the " room " they will not be visible to you. For a long time the house has been to let. Here, on the left of the doorway, as we enter, is the room, without a shred of furniture in it except the boards of two closed-in beds. The flooring is not steady, and here and there holes have been eaten into the planks. You can scarcely stand upright beneath the decaying ceiling. Worn boards and ragged walls, and the rusty ribs fallen from the fireplace, are all that meet your eyes, but I see a round, un-steady, waxcloth-covered table, with four books lying at equal distances on it. There are six prim chairs, two of them not to be sat upon, backed against the walls, and between the window and the fireplace a chest of drawers, with a snowy coverlet. On the drawers stands a board with coloured marbles for the game of solitaire, and I have only to open the drawer with the loose handle to bring out the dambrod. In the carved wood frame over the window hangs Jamie's portrait; in the only other frame a picture of Daniel in the den of lions, sewn by Leeby in wool. Over the chimney-piece with its shells, in which the roar of the sea can be heard, are strung three rows of birds' eggs. Once again we might be expecting company to tea.

The passage is narrow. There is a square hole between the rafters, and a ladder leading up to it. You may climb and look into the attic, as Jess liked to hear me call my tiny garret-room. I am stiffer now than in the days when I lodged with Jess during the summer holiday I am trying to bring back, and there is no need for me to ascend. Do not laugh at the newspapers with which Leeby papered the garret, nor at the yarn Hendry stuffed into the windy holes. He did it to warm the house for Jess. But the paper must have gone to pieces and the yarn rotted decades ago.

I have kept the kitchen for the last, as Jamie did on the dire day of which I shall have to tell. It has a flooring of stone now, where there used only to be hard earth, and a broken pane in the window is indifferently stuffed with rags. But it is the other window I turn to, with a pain at my heart, and pride and fondness too, the square foot of glass where Jess sat in her chair and looked down the brae.

Ah, that brae! The history of tragic little Thrums is sunk into it like the stones it swallows in the winter. We have all found the brae long

and steep in the spring of life. Do you remember
how the child you once were sat at the foot of it
and wondered if a new world began at the top ?
It climbs from a shallow burn, and we used to sit
on the brig a long time before venturing to climb
As boys we ran up the brae. As men and women,
young and in our prime, we almost forgot that it
was there. But the autumn of life comes, and the
brae grows steeper; then the winter, and once
again we are as the child pausing apprehensively
on the brig. Yet are we no longer the child; we
look now for no new world at the top, only for a
little garden and a tiny house, and a handloom in
the house. It is only a garden of kail and potatoes, but there may be a line of daisies, white and
red, on each side of the narrow footpath, and honey-
suckle over the door. Life is not always hard,
even after backs grow bent, and we know that all
braes lead only to the grave.

This is Jess's window. For more than twenty
years she had not been able to go so far as the
door, and only once while I knew her was she ben
in the room. With her husband, Hendry, or their
only daughter, Leeby, to lean upon, and her hand
clutching her staff, she took twice a day, when she
was strong, the journey between her bed and the
window where stood her chair. She did not lie
there looking at the sparrows or at Leeby redding
up the house, and I hardly ever heard her com-

plain. All the sewing was done by her; she often baked on a table pushed close to the window, and by leaning forward she could stir the porridge. Leeby was seldom off her feet, but I do not know that she did more than Jess, who liked to tell me, when she had a moment to spare, that she had a terrible lot to be thankful for.

To those who dwell in great cities Thrums is only a small place, but what a clatter of life it has for me when I come to it from my school-house in the glen. Had my lot been cast in a town I would no doubt have sought country parts during my September holiday, but the school-house is quiet even when the summer takes brakes full of sportsmen and others past the top of my footpath, and I was always light-hearted when Craigiebuckle's cart bore me into the din of Thrums. I only once stayed during the whole of my holiday at the house on the brae, but I knew its inmates for many years, including Jamie, the son, who was a barber in London. Of their ancestry I never heard. With us it was only some of the articles of furniture, or perhaps a snuff-mull, that had a genealogical tree. In the house on the brae was a great kettle, called the boiler, that was said to be fifty years old in the days of Hendry's grandfather, of whom nothing more is known. Jess's chair, which had carved arms and a seat stuffed with rags, had been Snecky Hobart's father's before it was hers.

and old Snecky bought it at a roup in the Tenements. Jess's rarest possession was, perhaps, the christening robe that even people at a distance came to borrow. Her mother could count up a hundred persons who had been baptized in it.

Every one of the hundred, I believe, is dead, and even I cannot now pick out Jess and Hendry's grave; but I heard recently that the christening robe is still in use. It is strange that I should still be left after so many changes, one of the three or four who can to-day stand on the brae and point out Jess's window. The little window commands the incline to the point where the brae suddenly jerks out of sight in its climb down into the town. The steep path up the commonty makes for this elbow of the brae, and thus, whichever way the traveller takes, it is here that he comes first into sight of the window. Here, too, those who go to the town from the south get their first glimpse of Thrums.

Carts pass up and down the brae every few minutes, and there comes an occasional gig. Seldom is the brae empty, for many live beyond the top of it now, and men and women go by to their work, children to school or play. Not one of the children I see from the window to-day is known to me, and most of the men and women I only recognize by their likeness to their parents. That sweet-faced old woman with the shawl on her shoulders may be one of the girls who was playing at the game of palaulays when Jamie stole into Thrums for the last time; the man who is leaning on the commonty gate gathering breath for the last quarter of the brae may, as a barefooted callant, have been one of those who chased Cree Queery past the poor-house. I cannot say; but this I know, that the grandparents of most of these boys and girls were once young with me. If I see the sons and daughters of my friends grown old, I also see the grandchildren spinning the peerie and hunkering at I-dree-I-dree — I-droppit-it — as we did so long ago. The world remains as young as ever. The lovers that met on the commonty in the gloaming are gone, but there are other lovers to take their place, and still the commonty is here. The sun had sunk on a fine day in June, early in the century, when Hendry and Jess, newly married, he in a rich moleskin waistcoat, she in a white net cap, walked to the house on the brae that was to be their home. So Jess has told me. Here again has been just such a day, and somewhere in Thrums there may be just such a couple, setting out for their home behind a horse with white ears instead of walking, but with the same hopes and fears, and the same love light in their eyes. The world does not age. The hearse passes over the brae and up the straight burying-ground road, but still there is a cry for the christening robe.

7

Jess's window was a beacon by night to travellers in the dark, and it will be so in the future when there are none to remember Jess. There are many such windows still, with loving faces behind them. From them we watch for the friends and relatives who are coming back, and some, alas! watch in vain. Not every one returns who takes the elbow of the brae bravely, or waves his handkerchief to those who watch from the window with wet eyes, and some return too late. To Jess, at her window always when she was not in bed, things happy and mournful and terrible came into view. At this window she sat for twenty years or more looking at the world as through a telescope; and here an awful ordeal was gone through after her sweet untarnished soul had been given back to God.

CHAPTER II

ON THE TRACK OF THE MINISTER

On the afternoon of the Saturday that carted me and my two boxes to Thrums, I was ben in the room playing Hendry at the dambrod. I had one of the room chairs, but Leeby brought a chair from the kitchen for her father. Our door stood open, and as Hendry often pondered for two minutes with his hand on a "man," I could have joined in the gossip that was going on but the house.

"Ay, weel, then, Leeby," said Jess, suddenly, "I'll warrant the minister 'll no be preachin' the morn."

This took Leeby to the window.

"Yea, yea," she said (and I knew she was nodding her head sagaciously); I looked out at the room window, but all I could see was a man wheeling an empty barrow down the brae.

"That's Robbie Tosh," continued Leeby; "an' there's nae doot 'at he's makkin for the minister's, for he has on his black coat. He'll be to row the minister's luggage to the post-cart. Ay, an' that's

9

Davit Lunnan's barrow. I ken it by the shaft's bein' spliced wi' yarn. Davit broke the shaft at the saw-mill."

"He'll be gaen awa for a curran (number of) days," said Jess, "or he would juist hae taen his bag. Ay, he'll be awa to Edinbory, to see the lass."

"I wonder wha'll be to preach the morn — tod, it'll likely be Mr. Skinner, frae Dundee; him an' the minister's chief, ye ken."

"Ye micht' gang up to the attic, Leeby, an' see if the spare bedroom vent (chimney) at the manse is gaen. We're sure, if it's Mr. Skinner, he'll come wi' the post frae Tilliedrum the nicht, an' sleep at the manse."

"Weel, I assure ye," said Leeby, descending from the attic, "it'll no be Mr. Skinner, for no only is the spare bedroom vent no gaen, but the blind's drawn doon frae tap to fut, so they're no even airin' the room. Na, it canna be him; an' what's mair, it'll be naebody 'at's to bide a' nicht at the manse."

"I wouldna say that; na, na. It may only be a student; an' Marget Dundas" (the minister's mother and housekeeper) "michtna think it necessary to put on a fire for him."

"Tod, I'll tell ye wha it'll be. I wonder I didna think o' 'im sooner. It'll be the lad Wilkie; him 'at's mither mairit on Sam'l Duthie's wife's brither.

They bide in Cupar, an' I mind 'at when the son was here twa or three year syne he was juist gaen to begin the diveenity classes in Glesca."

" If that's so, Leeby, he would be sure to bide wi' Sam'l. Hendry, hae ye heard 'at Sam'l Duthie's expeckin' a stranger the nicht ? "

" Haud yer tongue," replied Hendry, who was having the worst of the game.

" Ay, but I ken he is," said Leeby triumphantly to her mother, " for ye mind when I was in at Johnny Watt's (the draper's) Chirsty (Sam'l's wife) was buyin' twa yards o' chintz, an' I couldna think what she would be wantin' 't for ! "

" I thocht Johnny said to ye 'at it was for a present to Chirsty's auntie ? "

" Ay, but he juist guessed that; for, though he tried to get oot o' Chirsty what she wanted the chintz for, she wouldna tell 'im. But I see noo what she was after. The lad Wilkie 'll be to bide wi' them, and Chirsty had bocht the chintz to cover the airm-chair wi'. It's ane o' thae hair-bottomed chairs, but terrible torn, so she'll hae covered it for 'im to sit on."

" I wouldna wonder but ye're richt, Leeby; for Chirsty would be in an oncommon fluster if she thocht the lad's mither was likely to hear 'at her best chair was torn. Ay, ay, bein' a man, he wouldna think to tak off the chintz an' hae a look at the chair withoot it."

Here Hendry, who had paid no attention to the conversation, broke in —

"Was ye speirin' had I seen Sam'l Duthie? I saw 'im yesterday buyin' a fender at Will'um Crook's roup."

"A fe'der! Ay, ay, that settles the queistion," said Leeby; "I'll warrant the fender was for Chirsty's parlour. It's preyed on Chirsty's mind, they say, this fower-and-thirty year 'at she doesna hae a richt parlour fender."

"Leeby, look! That's Robbie Tosh wi' the barrow. He has a michty load o' luggage. Am thinkin' the minister's bound for Tilliedrum."

"Na, he's no, he's gaen to Edinbory, as ye micht ken by the bandbox. That'll be his mither's bonnet he's takkin' back to get altered. Ye'll mind she was never pleased wi' the set o' the flowers."

"Weel, weel, here comes the minister himsel, an' very snod he is. Ay, Marget's been puttin' new braid on his coat, an' he's carryin' the sma' black bag he bocht in Dundee last year: he'll hae's nicht-shirt an' a comb in't, I dinna doot. Ye micht rin to the corner, Leeby, an' see if he cries in at Jess McTaggart's in passin'."

"It's my opeenion," said Leeby, returning excitedly from the corner, "'at the lad Wilkie's no to be preachin' the morn, after a'. When I gangs to the corner, at ony rate, what think ye's the first

12

thing I see but the minister an' Sam'l Duthie meetin' face to face? Ay, weel, it's gospel am tellin' ye when I say as Sam'l flung back his head an' walkit richt by the minister!"

"Losh keep's a', Leeby; ye say that? They maun hae haen a quarrel."

"I'm thinkin' we'll hae Mr. Skinner i' the poopit the morn after a'."

"It may be, it may be. Ay, ay, look, Leeby, whatna bit kimmer's that wi' the twa jugs in her hand?"

"Eh? Ou, it'll be Lawyer Ogilvy's servant lassieky gaen to the farm o' T'nowhead for the milk. She gangs ilka Saturday nicht. But what did ye say — twa jugs? Tod, let's see! Ay, she has so, a big jug an' a little ane. The little ane 'll be for cream; an', sal, the big ane's bigger na usual."

"There maun be something gaen on at the lawyer's if they're buyin' cream, Leeby. Their reg'lar thing's twopence worth o' milk."

"Ay, but I assure ye that sma' jug's for cream, an' I dinna doot mysel but 'at there's to be fower-pence worth o' milk this nicht."

"There's to be a puddin' made the morn, Leeby. Ou, ay, a' thing points to that; an' we're very sure there's nae puddins at the lawyer's on the Sabbath onless they hae company."

"I dinna ken wha they can hae, if it be na that brither o' the wife's 'at bides oot by Aberdeen."

"Na, it's no him, Leeby; na, na. He's no weel to do, an' they wouldna be buyin' cream for 'im."

"I'll run up to the attic again, an' see if there's ony stir at the lawyer's hoose."

By and by Leeby returned in triumph.

"Ou, ay," she said, "they're expectin' veesitors at the lawyer's, for I could see twa o' the bairns dressed up to the nines, an' Mistress Ogilvy doesna dress at them in that wy for naething."

"It fair beats me though, Leeby, to guess wha's comin' to them. Ay, but stop a meenute, I wouldna wonder, no, really I would not wonder but what it'll be — "

"The very thing 'at was passin' through my head, mother."

"Ye mean 'at the lad Wilkie 'll be to bide wi' the lawyer i'stead o' wi' Sam'l Duthie? Sal, am thinkin' that's it. Ye ken Sam'l an' the lawyer married on cousins; but Mistress Ogilvy ay lookit on Chirsty as dirt aneath her feet. She would be glad to get a minister, though, to the hoose, an' so I warrant the lad Wilkie 'll be to bide a' nicht at the lawyer's."

"But what would Chirsty be doin' gettin' the chintz an' the fender in that case?"

"Ou, she'd been expeckin' the lad, of course. Sal, she'll be in a michty tantrum aboot this. I wouldna wonder though she gets Sam'l to gang ower to the U. P.'s."

Leeby went once more to the attic.

"Ye're wrang, mother," she cried out. "Wha-ever's to preach the morn is to bide at the manse, for the minister's servant's been at Baker Duff's buyin' short-bread — half a lippy, nae doot."

"Are ye sure o' that, Leeby?"

"Oh, am certain. The servant gaed in to Duff's the noo, an', as ye ken fine, the manse fowk doesna deal wi' him, except they're wantin' short-bread. He's Auld Kirk."

Leeby returned to the kitchen, and Jess sat for a time ruminating.

"The lad Wilkie," she said at last, triumphantly, " 'll be to bide at Lawyer Ogilvy's; but he'll be gaen to the manse the morn for a tea-dinner."

"But what," asked Leeby, "aboot the milk an' the cream for the lawyer's?"

"Ou, they'll be hae'n a puddin' for the supper the nicht. That's a michty genteel thing, I've heard."

It turned out that Jess was right in every particular.

CHAPTER III

PREPARING TO RECEIVE COMPANY

LEEBY was at the fire brandering a quarter of steak on the tongs, when the house was flung into consternation by Hendry's casual remark that he had seen Tibbie Mealmaker in the town with her man.

" The Lord preserv's ! " cried Leeby.

Jess looked quickly at the clock.

" Half fower ! " she said, excitedly.

" Then it canna be dune," said Leeby, falling despairingly into a chair, " for they may be here ony meenute."

" It's most michty," said Jess, turning on her husband, " 'at ye should tak a pleasure in bringin' this hoose to disgrace. Hoo did ye no tell's suner ? "

" I fair forgot," Hendry answered, " but what's a' yer steer ? "

Jess looked at me (she often did this) in a way that meant, " What a man is this I'm tied to ! "

" Steer ! " she exclaimed.   " Is't no time we was makkin' a steer ?   They'll be in for their tea ony meenute, an' the room no sae muckle as sweepit.

Ay, an' me lookin' like a sweep; an' Tibbie Mealmaker 'at's sae partikler genteel seein' you sic a sicht as ye are!'"

Jess shook Hendry out of his chair, while Leeby began to sweep with the one hand, and agitatedly to unbutton her wrapper with the other.

"She didna see me," said Hendry, sitting down forlornly on the table.

"Get aff that table!" cried Jess. "See haud o' the besom," she said to Leeby.

"For mercy's sake, mother," said Leeby, "gie yer face a dicht, an' put on a clean mutch."

"I'll open the door if they come afore you're ready," said Hendry, as Leeby pushed him against the dresser.

"Ye daur to speak aboot openin' the door, an' you sic a mess!" cried Jess, with pins in her mouth.

"Havers!" retorted Hendry. "A man canna be aye washin' at 'imsel."

Seeing that Hendry was as much in the way as myself, I invited him upstairs to the attic, whence we heard Jess and Leeby upbraiding each other shrilly. I was aware that the room was speckless; but for all that, Leeby was turning it upside down.

"She's aye ta'en like that," Hendry said to me, referring to his wife, "when she's expectin' company. Ay, it's a peety she canna tak things cannier."

"Tibbie Mealmaker must be some one of importance?" I asked.

"Ou, she's naething by the ord'nar'; but ye see she was mairit to a Tilliedrum man no lang syne, an' they're said to hae a michty grand establishment. Ay, they've a wardrobe spleet new; an' what think ye Tibbie wears ilka day?"

I shook my head.

"It was Chirsty Miller 'at put it through the toon," Henry continued. "Chirsty was in Tilliedrum last Teisday or Wednesday, an' Tibbie gae her a cup o' tea. Ay, weel, Tibbie telt Chirsty 'at she wears hose ilka day."

"Wears hose?"

"Ay. It's some michty grand kind o' stockin'. I never heard o't in this toon. Na, there's naebody in Thrums 'at wears hose."

"And who did Tibbie get?" I asked; for in Thrums they say, "Wha did she get?" and "Wha did he tak?"

"His name's Davit Curly. Ou, a crittur fu' o' maggots, an' nae great match, for he's juist the Tilliedrum bill-sticker."

At this moment Jess shouted from her chair (she was burnishing the society teapot as she spoke), "Mind, Hendry McQumpha, 'at upon nae condition are you to mention the bill-stickin' afore Tibbie!"

"Tibbie," Hendry explained to me, "is a terrible vain tid, an' doesna think the bill-stickin' genteel. Ay, they say 'at if she meets Davit in the street wi' his paste-pot an' the brush in his hands she pretends no to ken 'im."

Every time Jess paused to think she cried up orders, such as —

" Dinna call her Tibbie, mind ye.   Always address her as Mistress Curly."

" Shak' hands wi' baith o' them, an' say ye hope they're in the enjoyment o' guid health."

" Dinna put yer feet on the table."

" Mind, you're no' to mention 'at ye kent they were in the toon."

" When onybody passes ye yer tea say, ' Thank ye.' "

" Dinna stir yer tea as if ye was churnin' butter, nor let on 'at the scones is no our ain bakin'."

" If Tibbie says onything aboot the china yer no' to say 'at we dinna use it ilka day."

" Dinna lean back in the big chair, for it's broken, an' Leeby's gi'en it a lick o' glue this meenute."

" When Leeby gies ye a kick aneath the table that'll be a sign to ye to say grace."

Hendry looked at me apologetically while these instructions came up.

" I winna dive my head wi' sic nonsense," he said ; it's no' for a man body to be sae crammed fu' o' manners."

" Come awa doon," Jess shouted to him, " an' put on a clean dickey."

" I'll better do't to please her," said Hendry,

"though for my ain part I dinna like the feel o'
a dickey on week-days. Na, they mak's think
it's the Sabbath."

Ten minutes afterwards I went downstairs to
see how the preparations were progressing. Fresh
muslin curtains had been put up in the room.
The grand footstool, worked by Leeby, was so
placed that Tibbie could not help seeing it; and a
fine cambric handkerchief, of which Jess was very
proud, was hanging out of a drawer as if by accident. An antimacassar lying carelessly on the
seat of a chair concealed a rent in the horse-hair,
and the china ornaments on the mantelpiece were
so placed that they looked whole. Leeby's black
merino was hanging near the window in a good
light, and Jess's Sabbath bonnet, which was never
worn, occupied a nail beside it. The tea-things
stood on a tray in the kitchen bed, whence they
could be quickly brought into the room, just as if
they were always ready to be used daily. Leeby,
as yet in deshabille, was shaving her father at a
tremendous rate, and Jess, looking as fresh as a
daisy, was ready to receive the visitors. She was
peering through the tiny window-blind looking for
them.

"Be cautious, Leeby," Hendry was saying, when
Jess shook her hand at him. "Wheesht," she
whispered; "they're comin'."

Hendry was hustled into his Sabbath coat, and

then came a tap at the door, a very genteel tap. Jess nodded to Leeby, who softly shoved Hendry into the room.

The tap was repeated, but Leeby pushed her father into a chair and thrust Barrow's Sermons open into his hand. Then she stole but the house, and swiftly buttoned her wrapper, speaking to Jess by nods the while. There was a third knock, whereupon Jess said, in a loud, Englishy voice —

"Was that not a chap (knock) at the door?"

Hendry was about to reply, but she shook her fist at him. Next moment Leeby opened the door. I was upstairs, but I heard Jess say —

"Dear me, if it's not Mrs. Curly — and Mr. Curly! And hoo are ye? Come in, by. Wee this is, indeed, a pleasant surprise!"

CHAPTER IV

Jess had gone early to rest, and the door of her bed in the kitchen was pulled to. From her window I saw Hendry buying dulse.

Now and again the dulseman wheeled his slimy boxes to the top of the brae, and sat there stolidly on the shafts of his barrow. Many passed him by, but occasionally some one came to rest by his side. Unless the customer was loquacious, there was no bandying of words, and Hendry merely unbuttoned his east-trouser pocket, giving his body the angle at which the pocket could be most easily filled by the dulseman. He then deposited his half-penny, and moved on. Neither had spoken; yet in the country they would have roared their predictions about to-morrow to a ploughman half a field away.

Dulse is roasted by twisting it round the tongs fired to a red-heat, and the house was soon heavy with the smell of burning sea-weed. Leeby was at the dresser munching it from a broth-plate, while Hendry, on his knees at the fireplace, gingerly tore

22

off the blades of dulse that were sticking to the tongs, and licked his singed fingers.

"Whaur's yer mother?" he asked Leeby.

"Ou," said Leeby, "whaur would she be but in her bed?"

Hendry took the tongs to the door, and would have cleaned them himself, had not Leeby (who often talked his interfering ways over with her mother) torn them from his hands.

"Leeby!" cried Jess at that moment.

"Ay," answered Leeby, leisurely, not noticing, as I happened to do, that Jess spoke in an agitated voice.

"What is't?" asked Hendry, who liked to be told things.

He opened the door of the bed.

"Yer mother's no weel," he said to Leeby.

Leeby ran to the bed, and I went ben the house.

In another two minutes we were a group of four in the kitchen, staring vacantly. Death could not have startled us more, tapping thrice that quiet night on the window-pane.

"It's diphtheria!" said Jess, her hands trembling as she buttoned her wrapper.

She looked at me, and Leeby looked at me.

"It's no, it's no," cried Leeby, and her voice was as a fist shaken at my face. She blamed me for hesitating in my reply. But ever since this malady left me a lonely dominie for life, diphtheria has been a knockdown word for me. Jess had discovered a great white spot on her throat. I knew the symptoms.

"Is't dangerous?" asked Hendry, who once had a headache years before, and could still refer to it as a reminiscence.

"Them 'at has 't never recovers," said Jess, sitting down very quietly. A stick fell from the fire, and she bent forward to replace it.

"They do recover," cried Leeby, again turning angry eyes on me.

I could not face her; I had known so many who did not recover. She put her hand on her mother's shoulder.

"Mebbe ye would be better in yer bed," suggested Hendry.

No one spoke.

"When I had the headache," said Hendry, "I was better in my bed."

Leeby had taken Jess's hand — a worn old hand that had many a time gone out in love and kindness when younger hands were cold. Poets have sung and fighting men have done great deeds for hands that never had such a record.

"If ye could eat something," said Hendry, "I would gae to the flesher's for 't. I mind when I had the headache, hoo a small steak — "

"Gae awa for the doctor, rayther," broke in Leeby.

Jess started, for sufferers think there is less hope for them after the doctor has been called in to pronounce sentence.

" I winna hae the doctor," she said, anxiously.

In answer to Leeby's nods, Hendry slowly pulled out his boots from beneath the table, and sat looking at them, preparatory to putting them on. He was beginning at last to be a little scared, though his face did not show it.

" I winna hae ye," cried Jess, getting to her feet, " ga'en to the doctor's sic a sicht. Yer coat's a' yarn."

" Havers," said Hendry, but Jess became frantic.

I offered to go for the doctor, but while I was up-stairs looking for my bonnet I heard the door slam. Leeby had become impatient, and darted off herself, buttoning her jacket probably as she ran. When I returned to the kitchen, Jess and Hendry were still by the fire. Hendry was beating a charred stick into sparks, and his wife sat with her hands in her lap. I saw Hendry look at her once or twice, but he could think of nothing to say. His terms of endearment had died out thirty-nine years before with his courtship. He had forgotten the words. For his life he could not have crossed over to Jess and put his arm round her. Yet he was uneasy. His eyes wandered round the poorly lit room.

" Will ye hae a drink o' watter ? " he asked.

There was a sound of footsteps outside.

"That'll be him," said Hendry in a whisper.

Jess started to her feet, and told Hendry to help her ben the house.

The steps died away, but I fancied that Jess now highly strung, had gone into hiding, and I went after her. I was mistaken. She had lit the room lamp, turning the crack in the globe to the wall. The sheepskin hearthrug, which was generally carefully packed away beneath the bed, had been spread out before the empty fireplace, and Jess was on the arm-chair hurriedly putting on her grand black mutch with the pink flowers.

"I was juist makkin' mysel respectable," she said, but without life in her voice.

This was the only time I ever saw her in the room.

Leeby returned panting to say that the doctor might be expected in an hour. He was away among the hills.

The hour passed reluctantly. Leeby lit a fire ben the house, and then put on her Sabbath dress. She sat with her mother in the room. Never before had I seen Jess sit so quietly, for her way was to work until, as she said herself, she was ready "to fall into her bed."

Hendry wandered between the two rooms, always in the way when Leeby ran to the window to see if that was the doctor at last. He would stand gaping in the middle of the room for five minutes, then slowly withdraw to stand as drearily but the house. His face lengthened. At last he sat down by the kitchen fire, a Bible in his hand. It lay open on his knee, but he did not read much. He sat there with his legs outstretched, looking straight before him. I believe he saw Jess young again. His face was very solemn, and his mouth twitched. The fire sank into ashes unheeded.

I sat alone at my attic window for hours, waiting for the doctor. From the attic I could see nearly all Thrums, but, until very late, the night was dark, and the brae, except immediately before the door, was blurred and dim. A sheet of light canopied the square as long as a cheap Jack paraded his goods there. It was gone before the moon came out. Figures tramped, tramped up the brae, passed the house in shadow and stole silently on. A man or boy whistling seemed to fill the valley. The moon arrived too late to be of service to any wayfarer. Everybody in Thrums was asleep but ourselves, and the doctor who never came.

About midnight Hendry climbed the attic stair and joined me at the window. His hand was shaking as he pulled back the blind. I began to realize that his heart could still overflow.

"She's waur," he whispered, like one who had lost his voice.

For a long time he sat silently, his hand on the blind. He was so different from the Hendry I had known, that I felt myself in the presence of a strange man. His eyes were glazed with staring at the turn of the brae where the doctor must first come into sight. His breathing became heavier, till it was a gasp. Then I put my hand on his shoulder, and he stared at me.

"Nine-and-thirty years come June," he said, speaking to himself.

For this length of time, I knew, he and Jess had been married. He repeated the words at intervals.

"I mind—" he began, and stopped. He was thinking of the spring-time of Jess's life.

The night ended as we watched; then came the terrible moment that precedes the day—the moment known to shuddering watchers by sick-beds, when a chill wind cuts through the house, and the world without seems cold in death. It is as if the heart of the earth did not mean to continue beating.

"This is a fearsome nicht," Hendry said, hoarsely.

He turned to grope his way to the stairs, but suddenly went down on his knees to pray. . . .

There was a quick step outside. I arose in time to see the doctor on the brae. He tried the latch, but Leeby was there to show him in. The door of the room closed on him.

From the top of the stair I could see into the dark passage, and make out Hendry shaking at the door. I could hear the doctor's voice, but not the words he said. There was a painful silence, and then Leeby laughed joyously.

"It's gone," cried Jess; "the white spot's gone! Ye juist touched it, an' it's gone! Tell Hendry."

But Hendry did not need to be told. As Jess spoke I heard him say, huskily: "Thank God!" and then he tottered back to the kitchen. When the doctor left, Hendry was still on Jess's arm-chair, trembling like a man with the palsy. Ten minutes afterwards I was preparing for bed, when he cried up the stair —

"Come awa' doon."

I joined the family party in the room: Hendry was sitting close to Jess.

"Let us read," he said, firmly, " in the fourteenth of John."

CHAPTER V

AFTER the eight o'clock bell had rung, Hendry occasionally crossed over to the farm of T'nowhead and sat on the pig-sty. If no one joined him he scratched the pig, and returned home gradually. Here what was almost a club held informal meetings, at which two or four, or even half a dozen assembled to debate, when there was any one to start them. The meetings were only memorable when Tammas Haggart was in fettle, to pronounce judgments in his well-known sarcastic way. Sometimes we had got off the pig-sty to separate before Tammas was properly yoked. There we might remain a long time, planted round him like trees, for he was a mesmerising talker.

There was a pail belonging to the pig-sty, which some one would turn bottom upwards and sit upon if the attendance was unusually numerous. Tammas liked, however, to put a foot on it now and again in the full swing of a harangue, and when he paused for a sarcasm I have seen the pail kicked toward him. He had the wave of the arm

30

that is so convincing in argument, and such a natural way of asking questions, that an audience not used to public speaking might have thought he wanted them to reply. It is an undoubted fact, that when he went on the platform, at the time of the election, to heckle the Colonel, he paused in the middle of his questions to take a drink out of the tumbler of water which stood on the table. As soon as they saw what he was up to, the spectators raised a ringing cheer.

On concluding his perorations, Tammas sent his snuff-mull round, but we had our own way of passing him a vote of thanks. One of the company would express amazement at his gift of words, and the others would add, "Man, man," or "Ye cow, Tammas," or, "What a crittur ye are!" all which ejaculations meant the same thing. A new subject being thus ingeniously introduced, Tammas again put his foot on the pail.

"I tak no creedit," he said, modestly, on the evening, I remember, of Willie Pyatt's funeral, "in bein' able to speak wi' a sort o' faceelity on topics 'at I've made my ain."

"Ay," said T'nowhead, "but it's no the faceelity o' speakin' 'at taks me. There's Davit Lunan 'at can speak like as if he had learned it aff a paper, an' yet I canna thole 'im."

"Davit," said Hendry, "doesna speak in a wy 'at a body can follow 'im. He doesna gae even on. Jess says he's juist like a man ay at the cross-roads, an' no sure o' his wy. But the stock has words, an' no ilka body has that."

"If I was bidden to put Tammas's gift in a word," said T'nowhead, "I would say 'at he had a wy. That's what I would say."

"Weel, I suppose I have," Tammas admitted, "but, wy or no wy, I couldna put a point on my words if it wasna for my sense o' humour. Lads, humour's what gies the nip to speakin'."

"It's what maks ye a sarcesticist, Tammas," said Hendry; "but what I wonder at is yer sayin' the humorous things sae aisy like. Some says ye mak them up aforehand, but I ken that's no true."

"No only is't no true," said Tammas, "but it couldna be true. Them 'at says sic things, an', weel I ken you're meanin' Davit Lunan, hasna nae idea o' what humour is. It's a think 'at spouts oot o' its ain accord. Some of the maist humorous things I've ever said cam oot, as a body may say, by themsels."

"I suppose that's the case," said T'nowhead, "an' yet it maun be you 'at brings them up?"

"There's no nae doubt aboot its bein' the case," said Tammas, "for I've watched mysel often. There was a vara guid instance occurred sune after I married Easie. The Earl's son met me one day, aboot that time, i' the Tenements, and he didna ken 'at Chirsty was deid, an' I'd married again. 'Well, Haggart,' he says, in his frank wy, 'and how is your wife?' 'She's vara weel, sir,' I maks answer, 'but she's no the ane you mean.'"

"Na, he meant Chirsty," said Hendry.

"Is that a' the story?" asked T'nowhead.

Tammas had been looking at us queerly.

"There's no nane o' ye lauchin'," he said, "but I can assure ye the Earl's son gaed east the toon lauchin' like onything."

"But what was't he lauched at?"

"Ou," said Tammas, "a humorist doesna tell whaur the humour comes in."

"No, but when you said that, did you mean it to be humorous?"

"Am no sayin' I did, but as I've been tellin' ye, humour spouts oot by itsel."

"Ay, but do ye ken noo what the Earl's son gaed awa lauchin' at?"

Tammas hesitated.

"I dinna exactly see't," he confessed, "but that's no an oncommon thing. A humorist would often no ken 'at he was ane if it wasna by the wy he makes other fowk lauch. A body canna be expeckit baith to mak the joke an' to see't. Na, that would be doin' twa fowks' wark."

"Weel, that's reasonable enough, but I have often seen ye lauchin'," said Hendry, "lang afore other fowk lauched."

"Nae doubt," Tammas explained, "an' that's

because humour has twa sides, juist like a penny piece. When I say a humorous thing mysel I'm dependent on other fowk to tak note o' the humour o't, bein' mysel ta'en up wi' the makkin' o't. Ay, but there's things I see an' hear 'at maks me lauch, an' that's the other side o' humour."

" I never heard it put sae plain afore," said T'nowhead, " an', sal, am no nane sure but what am a humorist too."

"Na, na, no you, T'nowhead," said Tammas, hotly.

" Weel," continued the farmer, " I never set up for bein' a humorist, but I can juist assure ye 'at I lauch at queer things too. No lang syne I woke up i' my bed lauchin' like onything, an' Lisbeth thocht I wasna weel. It was something I dreamed 'at made me lauch, I couldna think what it was, but I laughed richt. Was that no fell like a humorist ? "

" That was neither here nor there," said Tammas. " Na, dreams dinna coont, for we're no responsible for them. Ay, an' what's mair, the mere lauchin's no the important side o' humour, even though ye hinna to be telt to lauch. The important side's the other side, the sayin' the humorous things. I'll tell ye what : the humorist's like a man firin' at a target — he doesna ken whether he hits or no till them at the target tells 'im."

" I would be of opeenion," said Hendry, who was

one of Tammas's most staunch admirers, "'at another mark o' the rale humorist was his seein' humour in all things?"

Tammas shook his head — a way he had when Hendry advanced theories.

"I dinna haud wi' that ava," he said. "I ken fine 'at Davit Lunan gaes aboot sayin' he sees humour in everything, but there's nae surer sign 'at he's no a genuine humorist. Na, the rale humorist kens vara weel 'at there's subjects withoot a spark o' humour in them. When a subject rises to the sublime it should be regairded philosophically, an' no humorously. Davit would lauch 'at the grandest thochts, whaur they only fill the true humorist wi' awe. I've found it necessary to rebuke 'im at times whaur his lauchin' was oot o' place. He pretended aince on this vara spot to see humour i' the origin o' cock-fightin'."

"Did he, man?" said Hendry; "I wasna here. But what is the origin o' cock-fechtin'?"

"It was a' i' the *Cheap Magazine*," said T'nowhead.

"Was I sayin' it wasna?" demanded Tammas. "It was through me readin' the account oot o' the *Cheap Magazine* 'at the discussion arose."

"But what said the *Cheapy* was the origin o' cock-fechtin'?"

"T'nowhead 'll tell ye," answered Tammas; "he says I dinna ken."

"I never said naething o' the kind," returned T'nowhead, indignantly; "I mind o' ye readin't oot fine."

"Ay, weel," said Tammas, "that's a' richt. Ou, the origin o' cock-fightin' gangs back to the time o' the Greek wars, a thoosand or twa years syne, mair or less. There was ane, Miltiades by name, 'at was the captain o' the Greek army, an' one day he led them doon the mountains to attack the biggest army 'at was ever gathered thegither."

"They were Persians," interposed T'nowhead.

"Are you tellin' the story, or am I?" asked Tammas. "I kent fine 'at they were Persians. Weel, Miltiades had the matter o' twenty thoosand men wi' im', and when they got to the foot o' the mountain, behold there was two cocks fechtin'."

"Man, man," said Hendry, "an' was there cocks in thae days?"

"Ondoubtedly," said Tammas, "or hoo could thae twa hae been fechtin'?"

"Ye have me there, Tammas," admitted Hendry. "Ye're perfectly richt."

"Ay, then," continued the stone-breaker, "when Miltiades saw the cocks at it wi' all their micht, he stopped the army and addressed it. 'Behold!' he cried, at the top o' his voice, 'these cocks do not fight for their household gods, nor for the monuments of their ancestors, nor for glory, nor for liberty, nor for their children, but only because the one will not give way unto the other.' "

" It was nobly said," declared Hendry; "na, cocks wouldna hae sae muckle understandin' as to fecht for thae things. I wouldna wonder but what it was some laddies 'at set them at ane another.'

" Hendry doesna see what Miltydes was after," said T'nowhead.

" Ye've taen't up wrang, Hendry," Tammas explained. " What Miltiades meant was 'at if cocks could fecht sae weel oot o' mere deviltry, surely the Greeks would fecht terrible for their gods an' their bairns an' the other things."

" I see, I see; but what was the monuments of their ancestors ? "

" Ou, that was the gravestanes they put up i' their kirkyards."

" I wonder the other billies would want to tak them awa. They would be a michty wecht."

" Ay, but they wanted them, an' nat'rally the Greeks stuck to the stanes they paid for."

" So, so, an' did Davit Lunan mak oot 'at there was humour in that ? "

" He do so. He said it was a humorous thing to think o' a hale army lookin' on at twa cocks fechtin'. I assure ye I telt 'im 'at I saw nae humour in't. It was ane o' the most impressive sichts ever seen by man, an' the Greeks was sae

inspired by what Miltiades said 'at they sweepit
the Persians oot o' their country."

We all agreed that Tammas's was the genuine
humour.

"An' an enviable possession it is," said Hendry.

"In a wy," admitted Tammas, "but no in a'
wys."

He hesitated, and then added in a low voice —

"As sure as death, Hendry, it sometimes taks
grip o' me i' the kirk itsel, an' I can hardly keep
frae lauchin'."

CHAPTER VI

DEAD THIS TWENTY YEARS

In the lustiness of youth there are many who cannot feel that they, too, will die. The first fear stops the heart. Even then they would keep death at arm's length by making believe to disown him. Loved ones are taken away, and the boy, the girl, will not speak of them, as if that made the conqueror's triumph the less. In time the fire in the breast burns low, and then in the last glow of the embers, it is sweeter to hold to what has been than to think of what may be.

Twenty years had passed since Joey ran down the brae to play. Jess, his mother, shook her staff fondly at him. A cart rumbled by, the driver nodding on the shaft. It rounded the corner and stopped suddenly, and then a woman screamed. A handful of men carried Joey's dead body to his mother, and that was the tragedy of Jess's life.

Twenty years ago, and still Jess sat at the window, and still she heard that woman scream. Every other living being had forgotten Joey; even to Hendry he was now scarcely a name, but there

39

were times when Jess's face quivered and her old
arms went out for her dead boy.

"God's will be done," she said, "but oh, I
grudged Him my bairn terrible sair. I dinna
want him back noo, an' ilka day is takkin' me
nearer to him, but for mony a lang year I grudged
him sair, sair. He was juist five minutes gone,
an' they brocht him back deid, my Joey."

On the Sabbath day Jess could not go to church,
and it was then, I think, that she was with Joey
most. There was often a blessed serenity on her
face when we returned, that only comes to those
who have risen from their knees with their prayers
answered. Then she was very close to the boy
who died. Long ago she could not look out from
her window upon the brae, but now it was her seat
in church. There on the Sabbath evenings she
sometimes talked to me of Joey.

"It's been a fine day," she would say, "juist like
that day. I thank the Lord for the sunshine noo,
but oh, I thocht at the time I couldna look at the
sun shinin' again."

"In all Thrums," she has told me, and I know
it to be true, "there's no a better man than
Hendry. There's them 'at's cleverer in the wys
o' the world, but my man, Hendry McQumpha,
never did naething in all his life 'at wasna weel
intended, an' though his words is common, it's to
the Lord he looks. I canna think but what

Hendry's pleasin' to God. Oh, I dinna ken what to say wi' thankfulness to Him when I mind hoo guid he's been to me. There's Leeby 'at I couldna hae done withoot, me bein sae silly (weak bodily), an' ay Leeby's stuck by me an' gien up her life, as ye micht say, for me. Jamie — "

But then Jess sometimes broke down.

"He's so far awa," she said, after a time, "an' aye when he gangs back to London after his holidays he has a fear he'll never see me again, but he's terrified to mention it, an' I juist ken by the wy he taks haud o' me, an' comes runnin' back to tak haud o' me again. I ken fine what he's thinkin', but I daurna speak.

"Guid is no word for what Jamie has been to me, but he wasna born till after Joey died. When we got Jamie, Hendry took to whistlin' again at the loom, an' Jamie juist filled Joey's place to him. Ay, but naebody could fill Joey's place to me. It's different to a man. A bairn's no the same to him, but a fell bit o' me was buried in my laddie's grave.

"Jamie an' Joey was never nane the same nature. It was aye something in a shop, Jamie wanted to be, an' he never cared muckle for his books, but Joey hankered after being a minister, young as he was, an' a minister Hendry an' me would hae done our best to mak him. Mony, mony a time after he came in frae the kirk on the

Sabbath he would stand up at this very window and wave his hands in a reverent way, juist like the minister. His first text was to be 'Thou God seest me.'

"Ye'll wonder at me, but I've sat here in the lang fore-nichts dreamin' 'at Joey was a grown man noo, an' 'at I was puttin' on my bonnet to come to the kirk to hear him preach. Even as far back as twenty years an' mair I wasna able to gang aboot, but Joey would say to me, 'We'll get a carriage to ye, mother, so 'at ye can come and hear me preach on " Thou God seest me."' He would say to me, 'It doesna do, mother, for the minister in the pulpit to nod to ony of the fowk, but I'll gie you a look an' ye'll ken it's me.' Oh, Joey, I would hae gien you a look too, an' ye would hae kent what I was thinkin'. He often said, 'Ye'll be proud o' me, will ye no, mother, when ye see me comin' sailin' alang to the pulpit in my gown?' So I would hae been proud o' him, an' I was proud to hear him speakin' o't. 'The other fowk,' he said, 'will be sittin' in their seats wonderin' what my text's to be, but you'll ken, mother, an' you'll turn up to " Thou God seest me," afore I gie oot the chapter.' Ay, but that day he was coffined, for all the minister prayed, I found it hard to say, 'Thou God seest me.' It's the text I like best noo, though, an' when Hendry an' Leeby is at the kirk, I turn't up often, often in the Bible.

I read frae the beginnin' o' the chapter, but when I come to 'Thou God seest me,' I stop. Na, it's no 'at there's ony rebellion to the Lord in my heart noo, for I ken He was lookin' doon when the cart gaed ower Joey, an' He wanted to tak my laddie to Himsel. But juist when I come to 'Thou God seest me,' I let the Book lie in my lap, for aince a body's sure o' that they're sure o' all. Ay, ye'll laugh, but I think, mebbe juist because I was his mother, 'at though Joey never lived to preach in a kirk, he's preached frae 'Thou God seest me' to me. I dinna ken 'at I would ever hae been sae sure o' that if it hadna been for him, an' so I think I see 'im sailin' doon to the pulpit juist as he said he would do. I seen him gien me the look he spoke o' — ay, he looks my wy first, an' I ken it's him. Naebody sees him but me, but I see him gien me the look he promised. He's so terrible near me, an' him dead, 'at wen my time comes I'll be rale willin' to go. I dinna say that to Jamie, because he all trembles; but I'm auld noo, an' I'm no nane loth to gang."

Jess's staff probably had a history before it became hers, for, as known to me, it was always old and black. If we studied them sufficiently we might discover that staves age perceptibly just as the hair turns grey. At the risk of being thought fanciful I dare to say that in inanimate objects, as in ourselves, there is honourable and shameful old age, and that to me Jess's staff was a symbol of the good, the true. It rested against her in the window, and she was so helpless without it when on her feet, that to those who saw much of her it was part of herself. The staff was very short, nearly a foot having been cut, as I think she once told me herself, from the original, of which to make a porridge thieval (or stick with which to stir porridge), and in moving Jess leant heavily on it. Had she stood erect it would not have touched the floor. This was the staff that Jess shook so joyfully at her boy the forenoon in May when he ran out to his death. Joey, however, was associated in Jess's memory with her staff in less painful ways. When she spoke of him she took the dwarf of a staff in her hands and looked at it softly.

"It's hard to me," she would say, "to believe 'at twa an' twenty years hae come and gone since the nicht Joey hod (hid) my staff. Ay, but Hendry was straucht in thae days by what he is noo, an' Jamie wasna born. Twa' an' twenty years come the back end o' the year, an' it wasna thocht 'at I could live through the winter. 'Ye'll no last mair than anither month, Jess,' was what my sister Bell said, when she came to see me, and yet here I am aye sittin' at my window, an' Bell's been i' the kirkyard this dozen years.

"Leeby was saxteen month younger than Joey,

an' mair quiet like. Her heart was juist set on helpin' aboot the hoose, an' though she was but fower year auld she could kindle the fire an' red up (clean up) the room. Leeby's been my savin' ever since she was fower year auld. Ay, but it was Joey 'at hung aboot me maist, an' he took notice 'at I wasna gaen out as I used to do. Since sune after my marriage I've needed the stick, but there was days 'at I could gang across the road an' sit on a stane. Joey kent there was something wrang when I had to gie that up, an' syne he noticed 'at I couldna even gang to the window unless Hendry kind o' carried me. Na, ye wouldna think 'at there could hae been days when Hendry did that, but he did. He was a sort o' ashamed if ony o' the neighbours saw him so affectionate like, but he was terrible taen up aboot me. His loom was doon at T'nowhead's Bell's father's, an' often he cam awa up to see if I was ony better. He didna lat on to the other weavers 'at he was comin' to see what like I was. Na, he juist said he'd forgotten a pirn, or his cruizey lamp, or ony thing. Ah, but he didna mak nae pretence o' no carin' for me aince he was inside the hoose. He came crawlin' to the bed no to wauken me if I was sleepin', an' mony a time I made belief 'at I was, juist to please him. It was an awfu' business on him to hae a young wife sae helpless, but he wasna the man to cast that at me. I mind o' sayin' to him one day in my bed, 'Ye made a poor bargain, Hendry, when ye took me.' But he says, 'Not one soul in Thrums 'll daur say that to me but yersel, Jess. Na, na, my dawty, you're the wuman o' my choice; there's juist one wuman i' the warld to me, an' that's you, my ain Jess.' Twa an' twenty years syne. Ay, Hendry called me fond like names, thae no everyday names. What a straucht man he was!

"The doctor had said he could do no more for me, an' Hendry was the only ane 'at didna gie me up. The bairns, of course, didna understan', and Joey would come into the bed an' play on the top o' me. Hendry would hae ta'en him awa, but I liked to hae 'im. Ye see, we war long married afore we had a bairn, an' though I couldna bear ony other weight on me, Joey didna hurt me, somehoo. I liked to hae 'im so close to me.

"It was through that 'at he came to bury my staff. I couldna help often thinkin' o' what like the hoose would be when I was gone, an' aboot Leeby an' Joey left so young. So, when I could say it without greetin', I said to Joey 'at I was goin' far awa, an' would he be a terrible guid laddie to his father and Leeby when I was gone? He aye juist said, 'Dinna gang, mother, dinna gang,' but one day Hendry came in frae his loom, and says Joey, 'Father, whaur's my mother gaen to, awa frae us?' I 'll never forget Hendry's face.

His mooth juist opened an' shut twa or three times, an' he walked quick ben to the room. I cried oot to him to come back, but he didna come, so I sent Joey for him. Joey came runnin' back to me sayin', 'Mother, mother, am awfu' fleid (frightened), for my father's greetin' sair."

"A' thae things took a haud o' Joey, an' he ended in gien us a fleg (fright). I was sleepin' ill at the time, an' Hendry was ben sleepin' in the room wi' Leeby, Joey bein' wi' me. Ay, weel, one nicht I woke up in the dark an' put oot my hand to 'im, an' he wasna there. I sat up wi' a terrible start, an' syne I kent by the cauld 'at the door maun be open. I cried oot quick to Hendry, but he was a soond sleeper, an' he didna hear me. Ay, I dinna ken hoo I did it, but I got ben to the room an' shook him up. I was near daft with fear when I saw Leeby wasna there either. Hendry couldna tak it in a' at aince, but sune he had his trousers on, an' he made me lie down on his bed. He said he wouldna move till I did it, or I wouldna hae dune it. As sune as he was oot o' the hoose crying their names I sat up in my bed listenin'. Sune I heard speakin', an' in a minute Leeby comes runnin' in to me, roarin' an' greetin'. She was barefeeted, and had juist her nichtgown on, an' her teeth was chatterin'. I took her into the bed, but it was an hour afore she could tell me onything, she was in sic a state.

"Sune after Hendry came in carryin' Joey. Joey was as naked as Leeby, and as cauld as lead, but he wasna greetin'. Instead o' that he was awfu' satisfied like, and for all Hendry threatened to lick him he wouldna tell what he an' Leeby had been doin'. He says, though, says he, ' Ye'll no gang awa noo, mother; no, ye'll bide noo.' My bonny laddie, I didna fathom him at the time.

"It was Leeby 'at I got it frae. Ye see, Joey had never seen me gaen ony gait withoot my staff, an' he thocht if he hod it I wouldna be able to gang awa. Ay, he planned it all oot, though he was but a bairn, an' lay watchin' me in my bed till I fell asleep. Syne he creepit oot o' the bed, an' got the staff, and gaed ben for Leeby. She was fleid, but he said it was the only wy to mak me 'at I couldna gang awa. It was juist ower there whaur thae cabbages is 'at he dug the hole wi' a spade, an' buried the staff. Hendry dug it up next mornin'."

CHAPTER VII

THE STATEMENT OF TIBBIE BIRSE

On a Thursday Pete Lownie was buried, and when Hendry returned from the funeral Jess asked if Davit Lunan had been there.

"Na," said Hendry, who was shut up in the closet-bed, taking off his blacks, "I heard tell he wasna bidden."

"Yea, yea," said Jess, nodding to me significantly. "Ay, weel," she added, "we'll be hae'n Tibbie ower here on Saturday to deave's (weary us) to death aboot it."

Tibbie, Davit's wife, was sister to Marget, Pete's widow, and she generally did visit Jess on Saturday night to talk about Marget, who was fast becoming one of the most fashionable persons in Thrums. Tibbie was hopelessly plebeian. She was none of your proud kind, and if I entered the kitchen when she was there she pretended not to see me, so that, if I chose, I might escape without speaking to the like of her. I always grabbed her hand, however, in a frank way.

49

On Saturday Tibbie made her appearance. From the rapidity of her walk, and the way she was sucking in her mouth, I knew that she had strange things to unfold. She had pinned a grey shawl about her shoulders, and wore a black mutch over her dangling grey curls.

"It's you, Tibbie," I heard Jess say, as the door opened.

Tibbie did not knock, not considering herself grand enough for ceremony, and indeed Jess would have resented her knocking. On the other hand, when Leeby visited Tibbie, she knocked as politely as if she were collecting for the precentor's present. All this showed that we were superior socially to Tibbie.

"Ay, hoo are ye, Jess?" Tibbie said.

"Muckle aboot it," answered Jess; "juist aff an' on; ay, an' hoo hae ye been yersel?"

"Ou," said Tibbie.

I wish I could write "ou" as Tibbie said it. With her it was usually a sentence in itself. Sometimes it was a mere bark, again it expressed indignation, surprise, rapture; it might be a check upon emotion or a way of leading up to it, and often it lasted for half a minute. In this instance it was, I should say, an intimation that if Jess was ready Tibbie would begin.

"So Pete Lownie's gone," said Jess, whom I could not see from ben the house. I had a good glimpse of Tibbie, however, through the open door-ways. She had the armchair on the south side, as she would have said, of the fireplace.

" He's awa," assented Tibbie, primly.

I heard the lid of the kettle dancing, and then came a prolonged " ou." Tibbie bent forward to whisper, and if she had anything terrible to tell I was glad of that, for when she whispered I heard her best. For a time only a murmur of words reached me, distant music with an " ou " now and again that fired Tibbie as the beating of his drum may rouse the martial spirit of a drummer. At last our visitor broke into an agitated whisper, and it was only when she stopped whispering, as she did now and again, that I ceased to hear her. Jess evidently put a question at times, but so politely (for she had on her best wrapper) that I did not catch a word.

" Though I should be struck deid this nicht," Tibbie whispered, and the sibilants hissed between her few remaining teeth, " I wasna sae muckle as speired to the layin' oot. There was Mysy Cruick-shanks there, an' Kitty Wobster 'at was nae friends to the corpse to speak o', but Marget passed by me, me 'at is her ain flesh an' blood, though it mayna be for the like o' me to say it. It's gospel truth, Jess, I tell ye, when I say 'at, for all I ken officially, as ye micht say, Pete Lownie may be weel and hearty this day. If I was to meet

Marget in the face I couldna say he was deid, though I ken 'at the wricht coffined him; na, an' what's mair, I wouldna gie Marget the satisfaction o' hearin' me say it. No, Jess, I tell ye, I dinna pertend to be on an equalty wi' Marget, but equalty or no equalty, a body has her feelings, an' lat on 'at I ken Pete's gone I will not. Eh? Ou, weel. . . .

"Na faags a'; na, na. I ken my place better than to gang near Marget. I dinna deny 'at she's grand by me, and her keeps a bakehoose o' her ain, an' glad am I to see her doin' sae weel, but let me tell ye this, Jess, 'Pride goeth before a fall.' Yes, it does, it's Scripture; ay, it's nae mak-up o' mine, it's Scripture. And this I will say, though kennin' my place, 'at Davit Lunan is as dainty a man as is in Thrums, an' there's no one 'at's better behaved at a bural, being particularly wise-like (presentable) in's blacks, an' them spleet new. Na, na, Jess, Davit may hae his faults an' tak a dram at times like anither, but he would shame naebody at a bural, an' Marget deleeberately insulted him, no speirin' him to Pete's. What's mair, when the minister cried in to see me yesterday, an' me on the floor washin', says he, 'So Marget's lost her man,' an' I said, 'Say ye so, nae?' for let on 'at I kent, and neither me at the laying oot nor Davit Lunan at the funeral, I would not.

"'David should hae gone to the funeral,' says

the minister, 'for I doubt not he was only omitted in the invitations by a mistake.'

"Ay, it was weel meant, but says I, Jess, says I. 'As lang as am livin' to tak chairge o' 'im, Davit Lunan gangs to nae burals 'at he's no bidden to. An' I tell ye,' I says to the minister, 'if there was one body 'at had a richt to be at the bural o' Pete Lownie, it was Davit Lunan, him bein' my man an' Marget my ain sister. Yes,' says I, though am no o' the boastin' kind, 'Davit had maist richt to be there next to Pete 'imsel'.' Ou, Jess. . . .

"This is no a maiter I like to speak aboot; na, I dinna care to mention it, but the neighbours is nat'rally ta'en up aboot it, and Chirsty Tosh was sayin' what I would wager 'at Marget hadna sent the minister to hint 'at Davit's bein' overlookit in the invitations was juist an accident? Losh, losh, Jess, to think 'at a woman could hae the michty assurance to mak a tool o' the very minister! But, sal, as far as that gangs, Marget would do it, an' gae twice to the kirk next Sabbath, too; but if she thinks she's to get ower me like that, she taks me for a bigger fule than I tak her for. Na, na, Marget, ye dinna draw my leg (deceive me). Ou, no. . . .

"Mind ye, Jess, I hae no desire to be friends wi' Marget. Naething could be farrer frae my wish than to hae helpit in the layin' oot o' Pete Lownie, an', I assure ye, Davit wasna keen to gang to the bural. 'If they dinna want me to their burals,' Davit says, 'they hae nae mair to do than to say sae. But I warn ye, Tibbie,' he says, 'if there's a bural frae this hoose, be it your bural, or be it my bural, not one o' the family o' Lownies casts their shadows upon the corp.' Thae was the very words Davit said to me as we watched the hearse frae the sky-licht. Ay, he bore up wonderfu', but he felt it, Jess — he felt it, as I could tell by his takkin' to drink again that very nicht. Jess, Jess. . . .

"Marget's getting waur an' waur? Ay, ye may say so, though I'll say naething agin her mysel. Of coorse am no on equalty wi' her, especially since she had the bell put up in her hoose. Ou, I hinna seen it mysel, na, I never gang near the hoose, an', as mony a body can tell ye, when I do hae to gang that wy I mak my feet my friend. Ay, but as I was sayin', Marget's sae grand noo 'at she has a bell in the house. As I understan', there's a rope in the wast room, an' when ye pu' it a bell rings in the east room. Weel, when Marget has company at their tea in the wast room, an' they need mair watter or scones or onything, she rises an' rings the bell. Syne Jean, the auldest lassie, gets up frae the table an' lifts the jug or the plates an' gaes awa ben to the east room for what's wanted. Ay, it's a wy o' doin' 'at's juist like the gentry, but I'll tell ye, Jess, Pete juist fair hated the soond o' that bell, an' there's them 'at says it was the death o' 'im. To think o' Marget ha'en sic an establishment!...

"Na, I hinna seen the mournin', I've heard o't. Na, if Marget doesna tell me naething, am no the kind to speir naething, an' though I'll be at the kirk the morn, I winna turn my heid to look at the mournin'. But it's fac as death I ken frae Janet McQuhatty 'at the bonnet's a' crape, and three yairds o' crape on the dress, the which Marget calls a costume. . . . Ay, I wouldna wonder but what it was hale watter the morn, for it looks michty like rain, an' if it is it'll serve Marget richt, an' mebbe bring doon her pride a wee. No 'at I want to see her humbled, for, in coorse, she's grand by the like o' me. Ou, but . . ."

CHAPTER VIII

A CLOAK WITH BEADS

On weekdays the women who passed the window were meagrely dressed; mothers in draggled winsey gowns, carrying infants that were armfuls of grandeur. The Sabbath clothed every one in her best, and then the women went by with their hands spread out. When I was with Hendry cloaks with beads were the fashion, and Jess sighed as she looked at them. They were known in Thrums as the Eleven and a Bits (threepenny bits), that being their price at Kyowowy's in the square. Kyowowy means finicky, and applied to the draper by general consent. No doubt it was very characteristic to call the cloaks by their market value. In the glen my scholars still talk of their schoolbooks as the tupenny, the fowerpenny, the saxpenny. They finish their education with the tenpenny.

Jess's opportunity for handling the garments that others of her sex could finger in shops was when she had guests to tea. Persons who merely dropped in and remained to tea got their meal, as a rule, in the kitchen. They had nothing on that Jess could not easily take in as she talked to them. But when they came by special invitation, the meal was served in the room, the guests' things being left on the kitchen bed. Jess not being able to go ben the house, had to be left with the things. When the time to go arrived, these were found on the bed, just as they had been placed there, but Jess could now tell Leeby whether they were imitation, why Bell Elshioner's feather went far round the bonnet, and Chirsty Lownie's reason for always holding her left arm fast against her side when she went abroad in the black jacket. Ever since My Hobart's eleven and a bit was left on the kitchen bed Jess had hungered for a cloak with beads. My's was the very marrows of the one T'nowhead's wife got in Dundee for ten-and-sixpence; indeed, we would have thought that 'Lisbeth's also came from Kyowowy's had not Sanders Elshioner's sister seen her go into the Dundee shop with T'nowhead (who was loth), and hung about to discover what she was after.

Hendry was not quick at reading faces like Tammas Haggart, but the wistful look on Jess's face when there was talk of eleven and a bits had its meaning for him.

" They're grand to look at, no doubt," I have heard him say to Jess, " but they're richt annoyin'.

That new wife o' Peter Dickie's had ane on in the kirk last Sabbath, an' wi' her sittin' juist afore us I couldna listen to the sermon for tryin' to count the beads."

Hendry made his way into these gossips un-invited, for his opinions on dress were considered contemptible, though he was worth consulting on material. Jess and Leeby discussed many things in his presence, confident that his ears were not doing their work; but every now and then it was discovered that he had been hearkening greedily. If the subject was dress, he might then become a little irritating.

"Oh, they're grand," Jess admitted; "they set a body aff oncommon."

"They would be no use to you," said Hendry, "for ye canna wear them except ootside."

"A body doesna buy cloaks to be wearin' at them steady," retorted Jess.

"No, no, but you could never wear yours though ye had ane."

"I dinna want ane. They're far ower grand for the like o' me."

"They're no nae sic thing. Am thinkin' ye're juist as fit to wear an eleven and a bit as My Hobart."

"Weel, mebbe I am, but it's oot o' the queistion gettin' ane, they're sic a price."

"Ay, an' though we had the siller, it would

surely be an awfu' like thing to buy a cloak 'at ye could never wear?"

" Ou, but I dinna want ane."

Jess spoke so mournfully that Hendry became enraged.

" It's most michty," he said, " 'at ye would gang an' set yer heart on sic a completely useless thing."

" I hinna set my heart on't."

" Dinna blether. Ye've been speakin' aboot thae eleven and a bits to Leeby, aff an' on, for twa month."

Then Hendry hobbled off to his loom, and Jess gave me a look which meant that men are trying at the best, once you are tied to them.

The cloaks continued to turn up in conversation, and Hendry poured scorn upon Jess's weakness, telling her she would be better employed mending his trousers than brooding over an eleven and a bit that would have to spend its life in a drawer. An outsider would have thought that Hendry was positively cruel to Jess. He seemed to take a delight in finding that she had neglected to sew a button on his waistcoat. His real joy, however, was the knowledge that she sewed as no other woman in Thrums could sew. Jess had a genius for making new garments out of old ones, and Hendry never tired of gloating over her cleverness so long as she was not present. He was always athirst for fresh proofs of it, and these were forth-coming every day. Sparing were his words of praise to herself, but in the evening he generally had a smoke with me in the attic, ard then the thought of Jess made him chuckle till his pipe went out. When he smoked he grunted as if in pain, though this really added to the enjoyment.

"It doesna matter," he would say to me, "what Jess turns her hand to, she can mak ony mortal thing. She doesna need nae teachin'; na, juist gie her a guid look at onything, be it clothes, or furniture, or in the bakin' line, it's all the same to her. She'll mak another exactly like it. Ye canna beat her. Her bannocks is so superior 'at a Tilliedrum woman took to her bed after tastin' them, an' when the lawyer has company his wife gets Jess to mak some bannocks for her an' syne pretends they're her ain bakin'. Ay, there's a story aboot that. One day the auld doctor, him 'at's deid, was at his tea at the lawyer's, an' says the guidwife, 'Try the cakes, Mr. Riach; they're my own bakin'.' Weel, he was a fearsomely outspoken man, the doctor, an' nae suner had he the bannock atween his teeth, for he didna stop to swallow't, than he says, 'Mistress Geddie,' says he, 'I wasna born on a Sabbath. Na, na, you're no the first grand leddy 'at has gien me bannocks as their ain bakin' 'at was baked and fired by Jess Logan, her 'at's Hendry McQumpha's wife.' Ay, they say the lawyer's wife didna ken which wy to look, she was that mortified. It's juist the same

wi' sewin'. There's wys o' ornamentin' christenin·
robes an' the like 'at's kent to naebody but hersel;
an' as for stockin's, weel, though I've seen her
mak sae mony, she amazes me yet. I mind o' a
furry waistcoat I aince had. Weel, when it was
fell dune, do you think she gae it awa to some
gaen aboot body (vagrant)? Na, she made it
into a richt neat coat to Jamie, wha was a bit laddie at the time. When he grew out o' it, she
made a slipbody o't for hersel. Ay, I dinna ken
a' the different things it became, but the last time
I saw it was ben in the room, whaur she'd covered
a footstool wi' 't. Yes, Jess is the cleverest crittur
I ever saw. Leeby's handy, but she's no a patch
on her mother."

I sometimes repeated these panegyrics to Jess.
She merely smiled, and said that the men haver
most terrible when they are not at their work.

Hendry tried Jess sorely over the cloaks, and a
time came when, only by exasperating her, could
he get her to reply to his sallies.

" Wha wants an eleven an' a bit?" she retorted
now and again.

" It's you 'at wants it," said Hendry, promptly.

" Did I ever say I wanted ane? What use
could I hae for't?"

" That's the queistion," said Hendry. " Ye
canna gang the length o' the door, so ye would
never be able to wear't."

"Ay, weel," replied Jess, "I'll never hae the chance o' no bein' able to wear't, for, hooever muckle I wanted it, I couldna get it."

Jess's infatuation had in time the effect of making Hendry uncomfortable. In the attic he delivered himself of such sentiments as these:

"There's nae understandin' a woman. There's Jess 'at hasna her equal for cleverness in Thrums, man or woman, an' yet she's fair skeered about thae cloaks. Aince a woman sets her mind on something to wear, she's mair onreasonable than the stupidest man. Ay, it micht mak them humble to see hoo foolish they are syne. No, but it doesna do't.

"If it was a thing to be useful noo, I wouldna think the same o't, but she could never wear't. She kens she could never wear't, an' yet she's juist as keen to hae't.

"I dinna like to see her so wantin' a thing, an' no able to get it. But it's an awfu' sum, eleven an' a bit."

He tried to argue with her further.

"If ye had eleven an' a bit to fling awa," he said, "ye dinna mean to tell me 'at ye would buy a cloak instead o' cloth for a gown, or flannel for petticoats, or some useful thing?"

"As sure as death," said Jess, with unwonted vehemence, "if a cloak I could get, a cloak I would buy."

Hendry came up to tell me what Jess had said.

"It's a michty infatooation," he said, "but it shows hoo her heart's set on thae cloaks."

"Aince ye had it," he argued with her, "ye would juist hae to lock it awa in the drawers. Ye would never even be seein' 't."

"Ay, would I," said Jess. "I would often tak it oot an' look at it. Ay, an' I would aye ken it was there."

"But naebody would ken ye had it but yersel," said Hendry, who had a vague notion that this was a telling objection.

"Would they no?" answered Jess. "It would be a' through the toon afore nicht."

"Weel, all I can say," said Hendry, "is 'at ye're terrible foolish to tak the want o' sic a useless thing to heart."

"Am no takkin' 't to heart," retorted Jess, as usual.

Jess needed many things in her days that poverty kept from her to the end, and the cloak was merely a luxury. She would soon have let it slip by as something unattainable had not Hendry encouraged it to rankle in her mind. I cannot say when he first determined that Jess should have a cloak, come the money as it liked, for he was too ashamed of his weakness to admit his project to me. I remember, however, his saying to Jess one day:

"I'll warrant you could mak a cloak yersel the

marrows o' thae eleven and a bits, at half the price?"

"It would cost," said Jess, "sax an' saxpence, exactly. The cloth would be five shillins, an' the beads a shillin'. I have some braid 'at would do fine for the front, but the buttons would be sax-pence."

"Ye're sure o' that?"

"I ken fine, for I got Leeby to price the things in the shop."

"Ay, but it maun be ill to shape the cloaks richt. There was a queer cut aboot that ane Peter Dickie's new wife had on."

"Queer cut or no queer cut," said Jess, "I took the shape o' My Hobart's ane the day she was here at her tea, an' I could mak the identical o't for sax and sax."

"I dinna believe't," said Hendry, but when he and I were alone he told me, "There's no a doubt she could mak it. Ye heard her say she had ta'en the shape? Ay, that shows she's rale set on a cloak."

Had Jess known that Hendry had been saving up for months to buy her material for a cloak, she would not have let him do it. She could not know, however, for all the time he was scraping together his pence, he kept up a ring-ding-dang about her folly. Hendry gave Jess all the wages he weaved, except threepence weekly, most of which went in tobacco and snuff. The dulseman had perhaps a halfpenny from him in the fortnight. I noticed that for a long time Hendry neither smoked nor snuffed, and I knew that for years he had carried a shilling in his snuff-mull. The remainder of the money he must have made by extra work at his loom, by working harder, for he could scarcely have worked longer.

It was one day shortly before Jamie's return to Thrums that Jess saw Hendry pass the house and go down the brae when he ought to have come in to his brose. She sat at the window watching for him, and by and by he reappeared, carrying a parcel.

"Whaur on earth hae ye been?" she asked, "an' what's that you're carryin'?"

"Did ye think it was an eleven an' a bit?" said Hendry.

"No, I didna," answered Jess, indignantly.

Then Hendry slowly undid the knots of the string with which the parcel was tied. He took off the brown paper.

"There's yer cloth," he said, "an' here's one an' saxpence for the beads an' the buttons."

While Jess still stared he followed me ben the house.

"It's a terrible haver," he said, apologetically, "but she had set her heart on't."

CHAPER IX

THE POWER OF BEAUTY

ONE evening there was such a gathering at the pig-sty that Hendry and I could not get a board to lay our backs against. Circumstances had pushed Pete Elshioner into the place of honour that belonged by right of mental powers to Tammas Haggart, and Tammas was sitting rather sullenly on the bucket, boring a hole in the pig with his sarcastic eye. Pete was passing round a card, and in time it reached me. "With Mr. and Mrs. David Alexander's compliments," was printed on it, and Pete leered triumphantly at us as it went the round.

"Weel, what think ye?" he asked, with a pretence at modesty.

"Ou," said T'nowhead, looking at the others like one who asked a question, "ou, I think; ay, ay."

The others seemed to agree with him, all but Tammas, who did not care to tie himself down to an opinion.

"Ou ay," T'nowhead continued, more confidently, "it is so, deceededly."

"Ye'll no ken," said Pete, chuckling, "what it means?"

"Na," the farmer admitted, "na, I canna say I exac'ly ken that."

"I ken, though," said Tammas, in his keen way.

"Weel, then, what is't?" demanded Pete, who had never properly come under Tammas's spell.

"I ken," said Tammas.

"Oot wi't then."

"I dinna say it's lyin' on my tongue," Tammas replied, in a tone of reproof, "but if ye'll juist speak awa aboot some other thing for a meenute or twa, I'll tell ye syne."

Hendry said that this was only reasonable, but we could think of no subject at the moment, so we only stared at Tammas, and waited.

"I fathomed it," he said at last, "as sune as my een lichted on't. It's one o' the bit cards 'at grand fowk slip 'aneath doors when they mak calls, an' their friends is no in. Ay, that's what it is."

"I dinna say ye're wrang," Pete answered, a little annoyed. "Ay, weel, lads, of course David Alexander's oor Dite as we called 'im, Dite Elshioner, an' that's his wy o' signifyin' to us 'at he's married."

"I assure ye," said Hendry, "Dite's doin' the thing in style."

"Ay, we said that when the card arrived," Pete admitted.

"I kent," said Tammas, "'at that was the wy grand fowk did when they got married. I've kent it a lang time. It's no nae surprise to me."

"He's been lang in marryin'," Hookey Crewe said.

"He was thirty at Martinmas," said Pete.

"Thirty, was he?" said Hookey. "Man, I'd buried twa wives by the time I was that age, an' was castin' aboot for a third."

"I mind o' them," Hendry interposed.

"Ay," Hookey said, "the first twa was angels." There he paused. "An' so's the third," he added, "in many respects."

"But wha's the woman Dite's ta'en?" T'nowhead or some one of the more silent members of the company asked of Pete.

"Ou, we dinna ken wha she is," answered Pete; "but she'll be some Glasca lassie, for he's there noo. Look, lads, look at this. He sent this at the same time; it's her picture." Pete produced the silhouette of a young lady, and handed it round.

"What do ye think?" he asked.

"I assure ye!" said Hookey.

"Sal," said Hendry, even more charmed, "Dite's done weel."

"Lat's see her in a better licht," said Tammas.

THE POWER OF BEAUTY

He stood up and examined the photograph narrowly, while Pete fidgeted with his legs.

"Fairish," said Tammas at last. "Ou, ay; no what I would selec' mysel, but a dainty bit stocky! Ou, a tasty crittury! ay, an' she's weel in order. Lads, she's a fine stoot kimmer."

"I conseeder her a beauty," said Pete, aggressively.

"She's a' that," said Hendry.

"A' I can say," said Hookey, "is 'at she taks me most michty."

"She's no a beauty," Tammas maintained; "na, she doesna juist come up to that; but I dinna deny but what she's weel faured."

"What faut do ye find wi' her, Tammas?" asked Hendry.

"Conseedered critically," said Tammas, holding the photograph at arm's length, "I would say 'at she — let's see noo; ay, I would say 'at she's defeecient in genteelity."

"Havers," said Pete.

"Na," said Tammas, "no when conseedered critically. Ye see she's drawn lauchin'; an' the genteel thing's no to lauch, but juist to put on a bit smirk. Ay, that's the genteel thing."

"A smile, they ca' it," interposed T'nowhead.

"I said a smile," continued Tammas. "Then there's her waist. I say naething agin her waist, speakin' in the ord'nar meanin'; but, conseedered critically, there's a want o' suppleness, as ye micht say, aboot it. Ay, it doesna compare wi' the waist o'——" (Here Tammas mentioned a young lady who had recently married into a local county family.)

"That was a pretty tiddy," said Hookey, "Ou, losh, ay! it made me a kind o' queery to look at her."

"Ye're ower kyowowy (particular), Tammas," said Pete.

"I may be, Pete," Tammas admitted; "but I maun say I'm fond o' a bonny-looken wuman, an' no aisy to please; na, I'm nat'rally ane o' the critical kind."

"It's extror'nar," said T'nowhead, "what a poo'er beauty has. I mind when I was a callant readin' aboot Mary Queen o' Scots till I was fair mad, lads; yes, I was fair mad at her bein'deid. Ou, I could hardly sleep at nichts for thinking o' her."

"Mary was spunky as weel as a beauty," said Hookey, "an' that's the kind I like. Lads, what a persuasive tid she was!"

"She got roond the men," said Hendry, "ay, she turned them roond her finger. That's the warst o' thae beauties."

"I dinna gainsay," said T'nowhead, "but what there was a little o' the deevil in Mary, the crittur."

Here T'nowhead chuckled, and then looked scared.

" What Mary needed," said Tammas, " was a strong man to manage her."

" Ay, man, but it's ill to manage thae beauties. They gie ye a glint o' their een, an' syne whaur are ye ? "

" Ah, they can be managed," said Tammas, complacently. " There's naebody nat'rally safter wi' a pretty stocky o' a bit wumany than mysel; but for a' that, if I had been Mary's man I would hae stood nane o' her tantrums. ' Na, Mary, my lass,' I would hae said, ' this winna do; na, na, ye're a bonny body, but ye maun mind 'at man's the superior; ay, man's the lord o' creation, an' so ye maun juist sing sma'.' That's hoo I would hae managed Mary, the speerity crittur 'at she was."

" Ye would hae haen yer wark cut oot for ye, Tammas."

" Ilka mornin'," pursued Tammas, " I would hae said to her, ' Mary,' I would hae said, ' wha's to wear thae breeks the day, you or me ? ' Ay, syne I would hae ordered her to kindle the fire, or if I had been the king, of coorse I would hae telt her instead to ring the bell an' hae the cloth laid for the breakfast. Ay, that's the wy to mak the like o' Mary respec ye."

Pete and I left them talking. He had written a letter to David Alexander, and wanted me to " back " it.

CHAPTER X

Two Bibles, a volume of sermons by the learned Dr. Isaac Barrow, a few numbers of the *Cheap Magazine*, that had strayed from Dunfermline, and a " Pilgrim's Progress," were the works that lay conspicuous ben in the room. Hendry had also a copy of Burns, whom he always quoted in the complete poem, and a collection of legends in song and prose, that Leeby kept out of sight in a drawer.

The weight of my box of books was a subject Hendry was very willing to shake his head over, but he never showed any desire to take off the lid. Jess, however, was more curious; indeed, she would have been an omnivorous devourer of books had it not been for her conviction that reading was idling. Until I found her out she never allowed to me that Leeby brought her my books one at a time. Some of them were novels, and Jess took about ten minutes to each. She confessed that what she read was only the last chapter, owing to a consuming curiosity to know whether "she got him."

She read all the London part, however, of " The

Heart of Midlothian," because London was where Jamie lived, and she and I had a discussion about it which ended in her remembering that Thrums once had an author of its own.

"Bring oot the book," she said to Leeby; "it was put awa i' the bottom drawer ben i' the room sax year syne, an' I sepad it's there yet."

Leeby came but with a faded little book, the title already rubbed from its shabby brown covers. I opened it, and then all at once I saw before me again the man who wrote and printed it and died. He came hobbling up the brae, so bent that his body was almost at right angles to his legs, and his broken silk hat was carefully brushed as in the days when Janet, his sister, lived. There he stood at the top of the brae, panting.

I was but a boy when Jimsy Duthie turned the corner of the brae for the last time, with a score of mourners behind him. While I knew him there was no Janet to run to the door to see if he was coming. So occupied was Jimsy with the great affair of his life, which was brewing for thirty years, that his neighbours saw how he missed his sister better than he realized it himself. Only his hat was no longer carefully brushed, and his coat hung awry, and there was sometimes little reason why he should go home to dinner. It is for the sake of Janet who adored him that we should remember Jimsy in the days before she died.

Jimsy was a poet, and for the space of thirty years he lived in a great epic on the Millennium. This is the book presented to me by Jess, that lies so quietly on my topmost shelf now. Open it, however, and you will find that the work is entitled "The Millennium: an Epic Poem, in Twelve Books: by James Duthie." In the little hole in his wall where Jimsy kept his books there was, I have no doubt — for his effects were rouped before I knew him except by name — a well-read copy of "Paradise Lost." Some people would smile, perhaps, if they read the two epics side by side, and others might sigh, for there is a great deal in "The Millennium" that Milton could take credit for. Jimsy had educated himself, after the idea of writing something that the world would not willingly let die came to him, and he began his book before his education was complete. So far as I know, he never wrote a line that had not to do with "The Millennium." He was ever a man sparing of his plural tenses, and "The Millennium" says "has" for "have"; a vain word, indeed, which Thrums would only have permitted as a poetical licence. The one original character in the poem is the devil, of whom Jimsy gives a picture that is startling and graphic, and received the approval of the Auld Licht minister.

By trade Jimsy was a printer, a master-printer with no one under him, and he printed and bound his book, ten copies in all, as well as wrote it. To print the poem took him, I dare say, nearly as long as to write it, and he set up the pages as they were written, one by one. The book is only printed on one side of the leaf, and each page was produced separately like a little hand-bill. Those who may pick up the book — but who will care to do so? — will think that the author or his printer could not spell — but they would not do Jimsy that injustice if they knew the circumstances in which it was produced. He had but a small stock of type, and on many occasions he ran out of a letter. The letter *e* tried him sorely. Those who knew him best said that he tried to think of words without an *e* in them, but when he was baffled he had to use a little *a* or an *o* instead. He could print correctly, but in the book there are a good many capital letters in the middle of words, and sometimes there is a note of interrogation after " alas " or " Woes me," because all the notes of exclamation had been used up.

Jimsy never cared to speak about his great poem even to his closest friends, but Janet told how he read it out to her, and that his whole body trembled with excitement while he raised his eyes to heaven as if asking for inspiration that would enable his voice to do justice to his writing. So grand it was, said Janet, that her stocking would slip from her fingers as he read — and Janet's stockings, that she was always knitting when not otherwise engaged, did not slip from her hands readily. After her death he was heard by his neighbours reciting the poem to himself, generally with his door locked. He is said to have declaimed part of it one still evening from the top of the commonty like one addressing a multitude, and the idlers who had crept up to jeer at him fell back when they saw his face. He walked through them, they told, with his old body straight once more, and a queer light playing on his face. His lips are moving as I see him turning the corner of the brae. So he passed from youth to old age, and all his life seemed a dream, except that part of it in which he was writing, or printing, or stitching, or binding " The Millennium." At last the work was completed.

" It is finished," he printed at the end of the last book. " The task of thirty years is over."

It is indeed over. No one ever read " The Millennium." I am not going to sentimentalize over my copy, for how much of it have I read? But neither shall I say that it was written to no end.

You may care to know the last of Jimsy, though in one sense he was blotted out when the last copy was bound. He had saved one hundred pounds by that time, and being now neither able to work nor to live alone, his friends cast about for a home for his remaining years. He was very spent and feeble, yet he had the fear that he might be still alive when all his money was gone. After that was the workhouse. He covered sheets of paper with calculations about how long the hundred pounds would last if he gave away for board and lodgings ten shillings, nine shillings, seven and sixpence a week. At last, with sore misgivings, he went to live with a family who took him for eight shillings. Less than a month afterwards he died.

CHAPTER XI

THE GHOST CRADLE

Our dinner-hour was twelve o'clock, and Hendry, for a not incomprehensible reason, called this meal his brose. Frequently, however, while I was there to share the expense, broth was put on the table, with beef to follow in clean plates, much to Hendry's distress, for the comfortable and usual practice was to eat the beef from the broth-plates. Jess, however, having three whole white plates and two cracked ones, insisted on the meals being taken genteelly, and her husband, with a look at me, gave way.

"Half a pound o' boiling beef, an' a penny bone," was Leeby's almost invariable order when she dealt with the flesher, and Jess had always neighbours poorer than herself who got a plateful of the broth. She never had anything without remembering some old body who would be the better of a little of it.

Among those who must have missed Jess sadly after she was gone was Johnny Proctor, a half-witted man who, because he could not work, remained straight at a time of life when most weavers, male and female, had lost some inches of their stature. For as far back as my memory goes, Johnny had got his brose three times a week from Jess, his custom being to walk in without ceremony, and, drawing a stool to the table, tell Leeby that he was now ready. One day, however, when I was in the garden putting some rings on a fishing-wand, Johnny pushed by me, with no sign of recognition on his face. I addressed him, and, after pausing undecidedly, he ignored me. When he came to the door, instead of flinging it open and walking in, he knocked primly, which surprised me so much that I followed him.

"Is this whaur Mistress McQumpha lives?" he asked, when Leeby, with a face ready to receive the minister himself, came at length to the door.

I knew that the gentility of the knock had taken both her and her mother aback.

"Hoots, Johnny," said Leeby, "what haver's this? Come awa in."

Johnny seemed annoyed.

"Is this whaur Mistress McQumpha lives?" he repeated.

"Say 'at it is," cried Jess, who was quicker in the uptake than her daughter.

"Of course this is whaur Mistress McQumpha lives," Leeby then said, "as weel ye ken, for ye had yer dinner here no twa hours syne."

"Then," said Johnny, "Mistress Tully's compliments to her, and would she kindly lend the christenin' robe, an' also the tea-tray, if the same be na needed?"

Having delivered his message as instructed, Johnny consented to sit down until the famous christening robe and the tray were ready, but he would not talk, for that was not in the bond. Jess's sweet face beamed over the compliment Mrs. Tully, known on ordinary occasions as Jean Mc-Taggart, had paid her, and, after Johnny had departed laden, she told me how the tray, which had a great bump in the middle, came into her possession.

"Ye've often heard me speak aboot the time when I was a lassie workin' at the farm o' the Bog? Ay, that was afore me an' Hendry kent ane anither, an' I was as fleet on my feet in thae days as Leeby is noo. It was Sam'l Fletcher 'at was the farmer, but he maun hae been gone afore you was mair than born. Mebbe, though, ye ken 'at he was a terrible invalid, an' for the hinmost years o' his life he sat in a muckle chair nicht an' day. Ay, when I took his denner to 'im, on that very tray 'at Johnny cam for, I little thocht 'at by an' by I would be sae keepit in a chair mysel.

"But the thinkin' o' Sam'l Fletcher's case is ane o' the things 'at maks me awfu' thankfu' for the lenient wy the Lord has aye dealt wi' me; for Sam'l couldna move oot o' the chair, aye sleepin in't at nicht, an' I can come an' gang between mine an' my bed. Mebbe, ye think I'm no much better off than Sam'l, but that's a terrible mistak. What a glory it would hae been to him if he could hae gone frae one end o' the kitchen to the ither. Ay, I'm sure o' that.

"Sam'l was rale weel liked, for he was saft-spoken to everybody, an' fond o' ha'en a gossip wi' ony ane 'at was aboot the farm. We didna care sae muckle for the wife, Eppie Lownie, for she managed the farm, an' she was fell hard an' terrible reserved we thocht, no even likin' ony body to get friendly wi' the mester, as we called Sam'l. Ay, we made a richt mistak."

As I had heard frequently of this queer, mournful mistake made by those who considered Sam'l unfortunate in his wife, I turned Jess on to the main line of her story.

"It was the ghost cradle, as they named it, 'at I meant to tell ye aboot. The Bog was a bigger farm in thae days than noo, but I daursay it has the new steadin' yet. Ay, it winna be new noo, but at the time there were sic a commotion aboot the ghost cradle, they were juist puttin' the new steadin' up. There was sax or mair masons at it, wi' the lads on the farm helpin', an' as they were all sleepin' at the farm, there was great stir aboot the place. I couldna tell ye hoo the story aboot the farm's bein' haunted rose, to begin wi', but I mind fine hoo fleid I was; ay, an' no only me, but every man-body an' woman-body on the farm. It was aye late 'at the soond began, an' we never saw naething, we juist heard it. The masons said they wouldna hae been sae fleid if they could hae seen't, but it never was seen. It had the soond o' a cradle rockin', an' when we lay in our beds hearkenin', it grew louder an' louder till it wasna to be borne, an' the women-folk fair skirled wi' fear. The mester was intimate wi' a' the stories aboot ghosts an water-kelpies an' sic like, an' we couldna help listenin' to them. But he aye said 'at ghosts 'at was juist heard an' no seen was the maist fearsome an' wicked. For all there was sic fear ower the hale farm-toon 'at naebody would gang ower the door alane after the gloamin' cam, the mester said he wasna fleid to sleep i' the kitchen by 'imsel. We thocht it richt brave o' 'im, for ye see he was as helpless as a bairn.

"Richt queer stories rose aboot the cradle, an' travelled to the ither farms. The wife didna like them ava, for it was said 'at there maun hae been some awful murder o' an infant on the farm, or we wouldna be haunted by a cradle. Syne folk began to mind 'at there had been na bairns born on the farm as far back as onybody kent, an' it was said 'at some lang syne crime had made the Bog cursed.

"Dinna think 'at we juist lay in our beds or sat round the fire shakkin' wi' fear. Everything 'at could be dune was dune. In the daytime, when naething was heard, the masons explored ae place i' the farm, in the hope o' findin' oot 'at the sound vas caused by sic a thing as the wind playin' on the wood in the garret. Even at nichts, when they couldna sleep wi' the soond, I've kent them rise in a body an' gang all ower the house wi' lichts. I've seen them climbin' on the new steadin', crawlin' alang the rafters, haudin' their cruizey lamps afore them, an' us women-bodies shiverin' wi' fear at the door. It was on ane o' thae nights 'at a mason fell off the rafters an' broke his leg. Weel, sic a state was the men in to find oot what it was 'at was ter-rifyin' them sae muckle, 'at the rest o' them climbed up at aince to the place he'd fallen frae, thinkin' there was something there 'at had fleid im. But though they crawled back an' forrit there was naething ava.

"The rockin' was louder, we thocht, after that nicht, an' syne the men said it would go on till somebody was killed. That idea took a richt haud o' them, an' twa ran awa back to Tilledrum, whaur they had come frae. They gaed thegither i' the middle o' the nicht, an' it was thocht next mornin' 'at the ghost had spirited them awa.

"Ye couldna conceive hoo low-spirited we all were after the masons had gien up hope o' findin' a nat'ral cause for the soond. At ord'nar times there's no ony mair lichtsome place than a farm after

the men hae come in to their supper, but at the
Bog we sat dour an' sullen; an' there wasna a mason or a farm-servant 'at would gang by 'imsel as
far as the end o' the hoose whaur the peats was
keepit. The mistress maun hae saved some siller
that spring through the Egyptians (gypsies) keepin'
awa, for the farm had got sic an ill name, 'at nae
tinkler would come near 't at nicht. The tailor-
man an' his laddie 'at should hae bidden wi' us
to sew things for the men, walkit off fair skeered
one mornin', an' settled doon at the farm o' Craigiebuckle fower mile awa, whaur our lads had to gae
to them. Ay, I mind the tailor's sendin' the laddie
for the money owin' him; he hadna the speerit to
venture again within soond o' the cradle 'imsel.
The men on the farm though, couldna blame 'im
for that. They were juist as flichtered themsels,
an' mony a time I saw them hittin' the dogs for
whinin' at the soond. The wy the dogs took on
was fearsome in itsel, for they seemed to ken, aye
when nicht cam on, 'at the rockin' would sune begin, an' if they werena chained they cam runnin'
to the hoose. I hae heard the hale glen fu, as
ye micht say, wi' the whinin' o' dogs, for the dogs
on the other farms took up the cry, an' in a glen
ye can hear soonds terrible far awa at nicht.

"As lang as we sat i' the kitchen, listenin' to
what the mester had to say aboot the ghosts in his
young days, the cradle would be still, but we were

nae suner awa speeritless to our beds than it began, an' sometimes it lasted till mornin.' We lookit upon the mester almost wi' awe, sittin' there sae helpless in his chair, an' no fleid to be left alane. He had lang white hair, an' a saft bonny face 'at would hae made 'im respeckit by onybody, an' aye when we speired if he wasna fleid to be left alane, he said, 'Them 'at has a clear conscience has naething to fear frae ghosts.'

"There was some 'at said the curse would never leave the farm till the house was razed to the ground, an' it's the truth I'm tellin' ye when I say there was talk among the men aboot settin 't on fire. The mester was richt stern when he heard o' that, quotin' frae Scripture in a solemn wy 'at abashed the masons, but he said 'at in his opeenion there was a bairn buried on the farm, an' till it was found the cradle would go on rockin'. After that the masons dug in a lot o' places lookin' for the body, an' they found some queer things, too, but never nae sign o' a murdered litlin'. Ay, I dinna ken what would hae happened if the commotion had gaen on muckle langer. One thing I'm sure o' is 'at the mistress would hae gaen daft, she took it a' sae terrible to heart.

"I lauch at it noo, but I tell ye I used to tak my heart to my bed in my mooth. If ye hinna heard the story I dinna think ye 'll be able to guess what the ghost cradle was."

I said I had been trying to think what the tray had to do with it.

"It had everything to do wi't," said Jess; "an' if the masons had kent hoo that cradle was rockit, I think they would hae killed the mester. It was Eppie 'at found oot, an' she telt naebody but me, though mony a ane kens noo. I see ye canna mak it oot yet, so I'll tell ye what the cradle was. The tray was keepit against the kitchen wall near the mester, 'an he played on't wi' his foot. He made it gang, bump bump, an' the soond was just like a cradle rockin'. Ye could hardly believe sic a thing would hae made that din, but it did, an' ye see we lay in our beds hearkenin' for't. Ay, when Eppie telt me, I could scarce believe 'at that guid devout-lookin' man could hae been sae wicked. Ye see, when he found hoo terrified we a' were, he keepit it up. The wy Eppie found out i' the tail o' the day was by wonderin' at 'im sleepin' sae muckle in the daytime. He did that so as to be fresh for his sport at nicht. What a fine releegious man we thocht 'im, too!

"Eppie couldna bear the very sicht o' the tray after that, an' she telt me to break it up; but I keepit it, ye see. The lump i' the middle's the mark, as ye may say, o' the auld man's foot."

CHAPTER XII

THE TRAGEDY OF A WIFE

WERE Jess still alive to tell the life-story of Sam'l Fletcher and his wife, you could not hear it and sit still. The ghost cradle is but a page from the black history of a woman who married, to be blotted out from that hour. One case of the kind I myself have known, of a woman so good mated to a man so selfish that I cannot think of her even now with a steady mouth. Hers was the tragedy of living on, more mournful than the tragedy that kills. In Thrums the weavers spoke of " lousing " from their looms, removing the chains, and there is something woeful in that. But pity poor Nanny Coutts, who took her chains to bed with her.

Nanny was buried a month or more before I came to the house on the brae, and even in Thrums the dead are seldom remembered for so long a time as that. But it was only after Sanders was left alone that we learned what a woman she had been, and how basely we had wronged her. She was an angel, Sanders went about whining when he had no longer a woman to ill-treat. He had this sentimental way with him, but it lost its effect after we knew the man.

"A deevil couldna hae deserved waur treatment," Tammas Haggart said to him; "gang oot o' my sicht, man."

"I'll blame mysel till I die," Jess said, with tears in her eyes, "for no understandin' puir Nanny better."

So Nanny got sympathy at last, but not until her forgiving soul had left her tortured body. There was many a kindly heart in Thrums that would have gone out to her in her lifetime, but we could not have loved her without upbraiding him, and she would not buy sympathy at the price. What a little story it is, and how few words are required to tell it ! He was a bad husband to her, and she kept it secret. That is Nanny's life summed up. It is all that was left behind when her coffin went down the brae. Did she love him to the end, or was she only doing what she thought her duty ? It is not for me even to guess. A good woman who suffers is altogether beyond man's reckoning. To such heights of self-sacrifice we cannot rise. It crushes us; it ought to crush us on to our knees. For us who saw Nanny, infirm, shrunken, and so weary, yet a type of the noblest womanhood, suffering for years, and misunderstood her to the end, what expiation can there be ? I do not want to storm at the man who made her life so burdensome. Too many years have passed for that, nor would Nanny take it kindly if I called her man names.

Sanders worked little after his marriage. He had a sore back, he said, which became a torture if he leant forward at his loom. What truth there was in this I cannot say, but not every weaver in Thrums could " louse " when his back grew sore. Nanny went to the loom in his place, filling as well as weaving, and he walked about, dressed better than the common, and with cheerful words for those who had time to listen. Nanny got no approval even for doing his work as well as her own, for they were understood to have money, and Sanders let us think her merely greedy. We drifted into his opinions.

Had Jess been one of those who could go about, she would, I think, have read Nanny better than the rest of us, for her intellect was bright, and always led her straight to her neighbours' hearts. But Nanny visited no one, and so Jess only knew her by hearsay. Nanny's standoffishness, as it was called, was not a popular virtue, and she was blamed still more for trying to keep her husband out of other people's houses. He was so frank and full of gossip, and she was so reserved. He would go everywhere, and she nowhere. He had been known to ask neighbours to tea, and she had shown that she wanted them away, or even begged them not to come. We were not accustomed to go behind the face of a thing, and so we set down Nanny's inhospitality to churlishness or greed. Only after her death, when other women had to attend him, did we get to know what a tyrant Sanders was at his own hearth. The ambition of Nanny's life was that we should never know it, that we should continue extolling him, and say what we chose about herself. She knew that if we went much about the house and saw how he treated her, Sanders would cease to be a respected man in Thrums.

So neat in his dress was Sanders, that he was seldom seen abroad in corduroys. His blue bonnet for everyday wear was such as even well-to-do farmers only wore at fair-time, and it was said that he had a handkerchief for every day in the week. Jess often held him up to Hendry as a model of courtesy and polite manners.

"Him an' Nanny's no weel matched," she used to say, "for he has grand ideas, an' she's o' the commonest. It maun be a richt trial to a man wi' his fine tastes to hae a wife 'at's wrapper's never even on, an' wha doesna wash her mutch aince in a month."

It is true that Nanny was a slattern, but only because she married into slavery. She was kept so busy washing and ironing for Sanders that she ceased to care how she looked herself. What did it matter whether her mutch was clean? Weaving and washing and cooking, doing the work of a breadwinner as well as of a housewife, hers was soon a body prematurely old, on which no wrapper would sit becomingly. Before her face, Sanders would hint that her slovenly ways and dress tried him sorely, and in company at least she only bowed her head. We were given to respecting those who worked hard, but Nanny, we thought, was a woman of means, and Sanders let us call her a miser. He was always anxious, he said, to be generous, but Nanny would not let him assist a starving child. They had really not a penny beyond what Nanny earned at the loom, and now we know how Sanders shook her if she did not earn enough. His vanity was responsible for the story about her wealth, and she would not have us think him vain.

Because she did so much, we said that she was as strong as a cart-horse. The doctor who attended her during the last week of her life discovered that she had never been well. Yet we had often wondered at her letting Sanders pit his own potatoes when he was so unable.

"Them 'at's strong, ye see," Sanders explained, "doesna ken what illness is, an' so it's nat'ral they shouldna sympathize wi' onweel fowk. Ay, I'm rale thankfu' 'at Nanny keeps her health. I often envy her."

These were considered creditable sentiments,

and so they might have been had Nanny uttered
them. Thus easily Saunders built up a reputation
for never complaining. I know now that he was
a hard and cruel man who should have married a
shrew; but while Nanny lived I thought he had
a beautiful nature. Many a time I have spoken
with him at Hendry's gate, and felt the better of
his heartiness.

"I mauna complain," he always said; "na, we
maun juist fecht awa."

Little, indeed, had he to complain of, and little
did he fight away.

Sanders went twice to church every Sabbath,
and thrice when he got the chance. There was
no man who joined so lustily in the singing or
looked straighter at the minister during the prayer.
I have heard the minister say that Sanders's con-
stant attendance was an encouragement and a help
to him. Nanny had been a great church-goer
when she was a maiden, but after her marriage she
only went in the afternoons, and a time came when
she ceased altogether to attend. The minister
admonished her many times, telling her, among
other things, that her irreligious ways were a distress to her husband. She never replied that she
could not go to church in the forenoon because
Sanders insisted on a hot meal being waiting him
when the service ended. But it was true that
Sanders, for appearance's sake, would have had

her go to church in the afternoons. It is now believed that on this point alone did she refuse to do as she was bidden. Nanny was very far from perfect, and the reason she forsook the kirk utterly was because she had no Sabbath clothes.

She died as she had lived, saying not a word when the minister, thinking it his duty, drew a cruel comparison between her life and her husband's.

"I got my first glimpse into the real state of affairs in that house," the doctor told me one night on the brae, "the day before she died 'You're sure there's no hope for me?' she asked wistfully, and when I had to tell the truth she sank back on the pillow with a look of joy."

Nanny died with a lie on her lips. "Ay," she said, "Sanders has been a guid man to me."

CHAPTER XIII

MAKING THE BEST OF IT

HENDRY had a way of resuming a conversation where he had left off the night before. He would revolve a topic in his mind, too, and then begin aloud, "He's a queer ane," or, "Say ye so?" which was at times perplexing. With the whole day before them, none of the family was inclined to waste strength in talk; but one morning when he was blowing the steam off his porridge, Hendry said, suddenly —

"He's hame again."

The women-folk gave him time to say to whom he was referring, which he occasionally did as an after-thought. But he began to sup his porridge, making eyes as it went steaming down his throat.

"I dinna ken wha ye mean," Jess said; while Leeby, who was on her knees rubbing the hearth-stone a bright blue, paused to catch her father's answer.

"Jeames Geogehan," replied Hendry, with the horn spoon in his mouth.

Leeby turned to Jess for enlightenment.

"Geogehan," repeated Jess; "what, no little Jeames 'at ran awa?"

"Ay, ay, but he's a muckle stoot man noo, an' gey grey."

"Ou, I dinna wonder at that. It's a guid forty year since he ran off."

"I waurant ye couldna say exact hoo lang syne 't is?"

Hendry asked this question because Jess was notorious for her memory, and he gloried in putting it to the test.

"Let's see," she said.

"But wha is he?" asked Leeby. "I never kent nae Geogehans in Thrums."

"Weel, it's forty-one years syne come Michaelmas," said Jess.

"Hoo do ye ken?"

"I ken fine. Ye mind his father had been lickin' 'im, an' he ran awa in a passion, cryin' oot 'at he would never come back? Ay, then, he had a pair o' boots on at the time, an' his father ran after 'im an' took them aff 'im. The boots was the last 'at Davie Mearns made, an' it's fully ane-an-forty years since Davie fell ower the quarry on the day o' the hill-market. That settles 't. Ay, an' Jeames 'll be turned fifty noo, for he was comin' on for ten year auld at that time. Ay, ay, an' he's come back. What a state Eppie 'll be in!"

"Tell's wha he is, mother."

"Od, he's Eppie Guthrie's son. Her man was William Geogehan, but he died afore you was born, an' as Jeames was their only bairn, the name o' Geogehan's been a kind o' lost sicht o'. Hae ye seen him, Hendry? Is't true 'at he made a fortune in thae far-awa countries? Eppie 'll be blawin' aboot him richt?"

"There's nae doubt aboot the siller," said Hendry, "for he drove in a carriage frae Tillie-drum, an' they say he needs a closet to hing his claes in, there's sic a heap o' them. Ay, but that's no a' he's brocht, na, far frae a'."

"Dinna gang awa till ye've telt's a' aboot 'im. What mair has he brocht?"

"He's brocht a wife," said Hendry, twisting his face curiously.

"There's naething surprisin' in that."

"Ay, but there is, though. Ye see, Eppie had a letter frae 'im no mony weeks syne, sayin' 'at he wasna deid, an' he was comin' hame wi' a fortune. He said, too, 'at he was a single man, an' she's been boastin' aboot that, so you may think 'at she got a surprise when he hands a wuman oot o' the carriage."

"An' no a pleasant ane," said Jess. "Had he been leein'?"

"Na, he was single when he wrote, an' single when he got the length o' Tilliedrum. Ye see, he fell in wi' the lassie there, an' juist gaed clean aft his heid aboot her. After managin' to withstand the women o' foreign lands for a' thae years, he gaed fair skeer aboot this stocky at Tilliedrum. She's juist seventeen years auld, an' the auld fule sits wi' his airm round her in Eppie's hoose, though they've been mairit this fortnicht."

" The doited fule," said Jess.

Jeames Geogehan and his bride became the talk of Thrums, and Jess saw them from her window several times. The first time she had only eyes for the jacket with fur round it worn by Mrs. Geogehan, but subsequently she took in Jeames.

" He's tryin' to carry't aff wi' his heid in the air," she said, " but I can see he's fell shamefaced, an' nae wonder. Ay, I'se uphaud he's mair ashamed o't in his heart than she is. It's an awful like thing o' a lassie to marry an auld man. She had dune't for the siller. Ay, there's pounds' worth o' fur aboot that jacket."

" They say she had siller hersel," said Tibbie Birse.

" Dinna tell me," said Jess. " I ken by her wy o' carryin' hersel 'at she never had a jacket like that afore."

Eppie was not the only person in Thrums whom this marriage enraged. Stories had long been alive of Jeames's fortune, which his cousins' children were some day to divide among themselves, and as a consequence these young men and women looked on Mrs. Geogehan as a thief.

"Dinna bring the wife to our hoose, Jeames," one of them told him, "for we would be fair ashamed to hae her. We used to hae a respect for yer name, so we couldna look her i' the face."

"She's mair like yer dochter than yer wife," said another.

"Na," said a third, "naebody could mistak her for yer dochter. She's ower young-like for that."

"Wi' the siller you'll leave her, Jeames," Tammas Haggart told him, "she'll get a younger man for her second venture."

All this was very trying to the newly-married man, who was thirsting for sympathy. Hendry was the person whom he took into his confidence.

"It may hae been foolish at my time o' life," Hendry reported him to have said, "but I couldna help it. If they juist kent her better they couldna but see 'at she's a terrible takkin' crittur."

Jeames was generous; indeed he had come home with the intention of scattering largess. A beggar met him one day on the brae, and got a shilling from him. She was waving her arms triumphantly as she passed Hendry's house, and Leeby got the story from her.

"Eh, he's a fine man that, an' a saft ane," the woman said. "I juist speired at 'im hoo his bonny wife was, an' he oot wi' a shillin'!"

Leeby did not keep this news to herself, and soon it was through the town. Jeames's face began to brighten.

"They're comin' round to a mair sensible wy o' lookin' at things," he told Hendry. "I was walkin' wi' the wife i' the buryin' ground yester-day, an' we met Kitty McQueen. She was ane o' the warst agin me at first, but she telt me i' the buryin' ground 'at when a man mairit he should please 'imsel. Oh, they're comin' round."

What Kitty told Jess was —

"I minded o' the tinkler wuman 'at he gae a shillin' to, so I thocht I would butter up at the auld fule too. Weel, I assure ye, I had nae suner said 'at he was rale wise to marry wha he likit than he slips a pound note into my hand. Ou, Jess, we've ta'en the wrang wy wi' Jeames. I've telt a' my bairns 'at if they meet him they're to praise the wife terrible, an' I'm far mista'en if that doesna mean five shillin's to ilka ane o' them."

Jean Whamond got a pound note for saying that Jeames's wife had an uncommon pretty voice, and Davit Lunan had ten shillings for a judicious word about her attractive manners. Tibbie Birse invited the newly-married couple to tea (one pound).

"They're takkin' to her, they're takkin' to her," Jeames said, gleefully. "I kent they would come round in time. Ay, even my mother, 'at was sae mad at first, sits for hours noo aside her, haudin' her hand. They're juist inseparable."

The time came when we had Mr. and Mrs. Geogehan and Eppie to tea.

"It's true enough," Leeby ran ben to tell Jess, "'at Eppie an' the wife's fond o' ane another. I wouldna hae believed it o' Eppie if I hadna seen it, but I assure ye they sat even at the tea-table haudin' ane another's hands. I waurant they're doin't this meenute."

"I wasna born on a Sabbath," retorted Jess. "Na, na, dinna tell me Eppie's fond o' her. Tell Eppie to come but to the kitchen when the tea's ower."

Jess and Eppie had half an hour's conversation alone, and then our guests left.

"It's a richt guid thing," said Hendry, "'at Eppie has ta'en sic a notion o' the wife."

"Ou, ay," said Jess.

Then Hendry hobbled out of the house.

"What said Eppie to ye?" Leeby asked her mother.

"Juist what I expeckit," Jess answered. "Ye see she's dependent on Jeames, so she has to butter up at 'im."

"Did she say onything aboot haudin' the wife's hand sae fond-like?"

"Ay, she said it was an awfu' trial to her, an' 'at it sickened her to see Jeames an' the wife baith believin' 'at she likit to do't."

CHAPTER XIV

VISITORS AT THE MANSE.

ON bringing home his bride, the minister showed her to us, and we thought she would do when she realized that she was not the minister. She was a grand lady from Edinburgh, though very frank, and we simple folk amused her a good deal, especially when we were sitting cowed in the manse parlour drinking a dish of tea with her, as happened to Leeby, her father, and me, three days before Jamie came home.

Leeby had refused to be drawn into conversation, like one who knew her place, yet all her actions were genteel and her monosyllabic replies in the Englishy tongue, as of one who was, after all, a little above the common. When the minister's wife asked her whether she took sugar and cream, she said politely, "If you please" (though she did not take sugar), a reply that contrasted with Hendry's equally well-intended answer to the same question. "I'm no partikler," was what Hendry said.

Hendry had left home glumly, declaring that

the white collar Jess had put on him would
throttle him; but her feikieness ended in his sur-
render, and he was looking unusually perjink.
Had not his daughter been present he would
have been the most at ease of the company, but her
manners were too fine not to make an impression
upon one who knew her on her every-day behav-
iour, and she had also ways of bringing Hendry
to himself by a touch beneath the table. It was
in church that Leeby brought to perfection her
manner of looking after her father. When he
had confidence in the preacher's soundness, he
would sometimes have slept in his pew if Leeby
had not had a watchful foot. She wakened him
in an instant, while still looking modestly at the
pulpit; however reverently he might try to fall
over, Leeby's foot went out. She was such an
artist that I never caught her in the act. All I
knew for certain was that, now and then, Hendry
suddenly sat up.

The ordeal was over when Leeby went upstairs
to put on her things. After tea Hendry had become bolder in talk, his subject being ministerial.
He had an extraordinary knowledge, got no one
knew where, of the matrimonial affairs of all the
ministers in these parts, and his stories about them
ended frequently with a chuckle. He always
took it for granted that a minister's marriage was
womanhood's great triumph, and that the par-

ticular woman who got him must be very clever. Some of his tales were even more curious than he thought them, such as the one Leeby tried to interrupt by saying we must be going.

"There's Mr. Pennycuick, noo," said Hendry, shaking his head in wonder at what he had to tell; "him 'at's minister at Tilliedrum. Weel, when he was a probationer he was michty poor, an' one day he was walkin' into Thrums frae Glen Quharity, an' he tak's a rest at a little housey on the road. The fowk didna ken him ava, but they saw he was a minister, an' the lassie was sorry to see him wi' sic an auld hat. What think ye she did?"

"Come away, father," said Leeby, re-entering the parlour; but Hendry was now in full pursuit of his story.

"I'll tell ye what she did," he continued. "She juist took his hat awa, an' put her father's new ane in its place, an' Mr. Pennycuick never kent the differ till he landed in Thrums. It was terrible kind o' her. Ay, but the old man would be in a michty rage when he found she had swappit the hats."

"Come away," said Leeby, still politely, though she was burning to tell her mother how Hendry had disgraced them.

"The minister," said Hendry, turning his back on Leeby, "didna forget the lassie. Na; as sune as he got a kirk, he married her. Ay, she got her reward. He married her. It was rale noble of 'im."

I do not know what Leeby said to Hendry when she got him beyond the manse gate, for I stayed behind to talk to the minister. As it turned out, the minister's wife did most of the talking, smiling good-humouredly at country gawkiness the while.

"Yes," she said, "I am sure I shall like Thrums, though those teas to the congregation are a little trying. Do you know, Thrums is the only place I was ever in where it struck me that the men are cleverer than the women."

She told us why.

"Well, to-night affords a case in point. Mr. McQumpha was quite brilliant, was he not, in comparison with his daughter? Really she seemed so put out at being at the manse that she could not raise her eyes. I question if she would know me again, and I am sure she sat in the room as one blindfolded. I left her in the bedroom a minute, and I assure you, when I returned she was still standing on the same spot in the centre of the floor."

I pointed out that Leeby had been awestruck.

"I suppose so," she said; "but it is a pity she cannot make use of her eyes, if not of her tongue. Ah, the Thrums women are good, I believe, but their wits are sadly in need of sharpening. I daresay it comes of living in so small a place."

I overtook Leeby on the brae, aware, as I saw her alone, that it had been her father whom I passed talking to Tammas Haggart in the Square. Hendry stopped to have what he called a tove with any likely person he encountered, and, indeed, though he and I often took a walk on Saturdays, I generally lost him before we were clear of the town.

In a few moments Leeby and I were at home to give Jess the news.

"Whaur's yer father?" asked Jess, as if Hendry's way of dropping behind was still unknown to her.

"Ou, I left him speakin' to Gavin Birse," said Leeby. "I daursay he's awa to some hoose."

"It's no very silvendy (safe) his comin' ower the brae by himsel," said Jess, adding in a bitter tone of conviction, "but he'll gang in to no hoose as lang as he's so weel dressed. Na, he would think it boastfu'."

I sat down to a book by the kitchen fire; but, as Leeby became communicative, I read less and less. While she spoke she was baking bannocks with all the might of her, and Jess, leaning forward in her chair, was arranging them in a semicircle round the fire.

"Na," was the first remark of Leeby's that

came between me and my book, "it is no new furniture."

"But there was three cart-loads o't, Leeby, sent on frae Edinbory. Tibbie Birse helpit to lift it in, and she said the parlour furniture beat a'."

"Ou, it's substantial, but it is no new. I sepad it had been bocht cheap second-hand, for the chair I had was terrible scratched like, an', what's mair, the airm-chair was a heap shinnier than the rest."

"Ay, ay, I wager it had been new stuffed. Tibbie said the carpet cowed for grandeur?"

"Oh, I dinna deny it's a guid carpet; but if it's been turned once it's been turned half a dozen times, so it's far frae new. Ay, an' forby, it was rale threadbare aneath the table, so ye may be sure they've been cuttin't an' puttin' the worn pairt whaur it would be least seen."

"They say 'at there's twa grand gas brackets i' the parlour, an' a wonderfu' gasoliery i' the dinin'-room?"

"We wasna i' the dinin'-room, so I ken naething aboot the gasoliery; but I'll tell ye what the gas brackets is. I recognized them immeditly. Ye mind the auld gasoliery i' the dinin'-room had twa lichts? Ay, then, the parlour brackets is made oot o' the auld gasoliery."

"Weel, Leeby, as sure as ye're standin' there, that passed through my head as sune as Tibbie mentioned them!"

"There's nae doot about it. Ay, I was in ane o' the bedrooms, too!"

"It would be grand?"

"I wouldna say 'at it was partikler grand, but there was a great mask (quantity) o' things in't, an' near everything was covered wi' cretonne. But the chairs dinna match. There was a very bonny-painted cloth alang the chimley — what they call a mantelpiece border, I warrant."

"Sal, I've often wondered what they was."

"Well, I assure ye they winna be ill to mak, for the border was juist nailed upon a board laid on the chimley. There's naething to hender's makin' ane for the room."

"Ay, we could sew something on the border instead o' paintin't. The room lookit weel, ye say?"

"Yes, but it was economically furnished. There was nae carpet below the wax-cloth; na, there was nane below the bed either."

"Was't a grand bed?"

"It had a fell lot o' brass aboot it, but there was juist one pair o' blankets. I thocht it was gey shabby, hae'n the ewer a different pattern frae the basin; ay, an' there was juist a poker in the fireplace, there was nae tangs."

"Yea, yea; they'll hae but one set o' bedroom fireirons. The tangs'll be in anither room. Tod, that's no sae michty grand for Edinbory. What like was she hersel?"

"Ou, very ladylike and saft spoken. She's a canty body an' frank. She wears her hair low on the left side to hod (hide) a scar, an' there's twa warts on her richt hand."

"There hadna been a fire i' the parlour?"

"No, but it was ready to licht. There was sticks and paper in't. The paper was oot o' a dressmaker's journal."

"Ye say so? She'll mak her ain frocks, I sepad."

When Hendry entered to take off his collar and coat before sitting down to his evening meal of hot water, porter, and bread mixed in a bowl, Jess sent me off to the attic. As I climbed the stairs I remembered that the minister's wife thought Leeby in need of sharpening.

CHAPTER XV

In a wet day the rain gathered in blobs on the road that passed our garden. Then it crawled into the cart-tracks until the road was streaked with water. Lastly, the water gathered in heavy yellow pools. If the on-ding still continued, clods of earth toppled from the garden dyke into the ditch.

On such a day, when even the dulseman had gone into shelter, and the women scudded by with their wrappers over their heads, came Gavin Birse to our door. Gavin, who was the Glen Quharity post, was still young, but had never been quite the same man since some amateurs in the glen ironed his back for rheumatism. I thought he had called to have a crack with me. He sent his compliments up to the attic, however, by Leeby, and would I come and be a witness?

Gavin came up and explained. He had taken off his scarf and thrust it into his pocket, lest the rain should take the colour out of it. His boots cheeped, and his shoulders had risen to his ears. He stood steaming before my fire.

" If it's no' ower muckle to ask ye," he said, " I would like ye for a witness."

" A witness! But for what do you need a witness, Gavin? "

" I want ye," he said, " to come wi' me to Mag's, and be a witness."

Gavin and Mag Birse had been engaged for a year or more. Mag was the daughter of Janet Ogilvy, who was best remembered as the body that took the hill (that is, wandered about it) for twelve hours on the day Mr. Dishart, the Auld Licht minister, accepted a call to another church.

" You don't mean to tell me, Gavin," I asked, " that your marriage is to take place to-day? "

By the twist of his mouth I saw that he was only deferring a smile.

" Far frae that," he said.

" Ah, then, you have quarrelled, and I am to speak up for you? "

" Na, na," he said, " I dinna want ye to do that above all things. It would be a favour if ye could gie me a bad character."

This beat me, and, I daresay, my face showed it.

" I'm no' juist what ye would call anxious to marry Mag noo," said Gavin, without a tremor.

I told him to go on.

" There's a lassie oot at Craigiebuckle," he explained, " workin' on the farm — Jeanie Luke by name. Ye may ha'e seen her? "

" What of her ? " I asked, severely.

" Weel," said Gavin, still unabashed, " I'm thinkin' noo 'at I would rather ha'e her."

Then he stated his case more fully.

" Ay, I thocht I liked Mag oncommon till I saw Jeanie, an' I like her fine yet, but I prefer the other ane. That state o' matters canna gang on for ever, so I came into Thrums the day to settle 't one wy or another."

" And how," I asked, " do you propose going about it ? It is a somewhat delicate business."

" Ou, I see nae great difficulty in 't. I'll speir at Mag, blunt oot, if she'll let me aff. Yes, I'll put it to her plain."

" You're sure Jeanie would take you ? "

" Ay ; oh, there's nae fear o' that."

" But if Mag keeps you to your bargain ? "

" Weel, in that case there's nae harm done."

" You are in a great hurry, Gavin ? "

" Ye may say that ; but I want to be married. The wifie I lodge wi' canna last lang, an' I would like to settle doon in some place."

" So you are on your way to Mag's now ? "

" Ay, we'll get her in atween twal' and ane."

" Oh, yes ; but why do you want me to go with you ? "

" I want ye for a witness. If she winna let me aff, weel and guid ; and if she will, it's better to hae a witness in case she should go back on her word."

Gavin made his proposal briskly, and as coolly as if he were only asking me to go fishing; but I did not accompany him to Mag's. He left the house to look for another witness, and about an hour afterwards Jess saw him pass with Tammas Haggart. Tammas cried in during the evening to tell us how the mission prospered.

" Mind ye," said Tammas, a drop of water hanging to the point of his nose, " I disclaim all responsibility in the business. I ken Mag weel for a thrifty, respectable woman, as her mither was afore her, and so I said to Gavin when he came to speir me."

" Ay, mony a pirn has 'Lisbeth filled to me," said Hendry, settling down to a reminiscence.

" No to be ower hard on Gavin," continued Tammas, forestalling Hendry, " he took what I said in guid part; but aye when I stopped speakin' to draw breath, he says, ' The queistion is, will ye come wi' me ? ' He was michty made up in 's mind."

" Weel, ye went wi' him," suggested Jess, who wanted to bring Tammas to the point.

" Ay," said the stone-breaker, " but no in sic a hurry as that."

He worked his mouth round and round, to clear the course, as it were, for a sarcasm.

" Fowk often say," he continued, " 'at 'am quick beyond the ordinar' in seeing the humorous side o' things."

Here Tammas paused, and looked at us.

"So ye are, Tammas," said Hendry. "Losh, ye mind hoo ye saw the humorous side o' me wearin' a pair o' boots 'at wisna marrows! No, the ane had a toe-piece on, an' the other hadna."

"Ye juist wore them sometimes when ye was delvin'," broke in Jess, "ye have as guid a pair o' boots as ony in Thrums."

"Ay, but I had worn them," said Hendry, "at odd times for mair than a year, an' I had never seen the humorous side o' them. Weel, as fac as death (here he addressed me), Tammas had juist seen them twa or three times when he saw the humorous side o' them. Syne I saw their humorous side, too, but no till Tammas pointed it oot."

"That was naething," said Tammas, "naething ava to some things I've done."

"But what aboot Mag?" said Leeby.

"We wasna that length, was we?" said Tammas. "Na, we was speakin' aboot the humorous side. Ay, wait a wee, I didna mention the humorous side for naething."

He paused to reflect.

"Oh, yes," he said at last, brightening up, "I was sayin' to ye hoo quick I was to see the humorous side o' onything. Ay, then, what made me say that was 'at in a clink (flash) I saw the humorous side o' Gavin's position."

"Man, man," said Hendry, admiringly, "and what is 't?"

"Oh, it's this, there's something humorous in speirin' a woman to let ye aff so as ye can be married to another woman."

"I daursay there is," said Hendry, doubtfully.

"Did she let him aff?" asked Jess, taking the words out of Leeby's mouth.

"I'm comin' to that," said Tammas. "Gavin proposes to me after I had haen my laugh —"

"Yes," cried Hendry, banging the table with his fist, "it has a humorous side. Ye're richt again, Tammas."

"I wish ye wadna blatter (beat) the table," said Jess, and then Tammas proceeded.

"Gavin wanted me to tak' paper an' ink an' a pen wi' me, to write the proceedins doon, but I said, 'Na, na, I'll tak' paper, but no nae ink nor nae pen, for there'll be ink an' a pen there.' That was what I said."

"An' did she let him aff?" asked Leeby.

"Weel," said Tammas, "aff we goes to Mag's hoose, an' sure enough Mag was in. She was alone, too; so Gavin, no to waste time, juist sat doon for politeness' sake, an' syne rises up again; an says he, 'Marget Lownie, I hae a solemn question to speir at ye, namely this, Will you, Marget Lownie, let me, Gavin Birse, aff?'"

"Mag would start at that?"

"Sal, she was braw an' cool. I thocht she maun ha'e got wind o' his intentions aforehand, for she juist replies, quiet-like, 'Hoo do ye want aff, Gavin?'

"'Because,' says he, like a book, 'my affections has undergone a change.'

"'Ye mean Jean Luke,' says Mag.

"'That is wha I mean,' says Gavin, very strait-forrard."

" But she didna let him aff, did she ? "

" Na, she wasna the kind.   Says she, ' I wonder to hear ye, Gavin, but 'am no goin' to agree to naething o' that sort.'

"'Think it ower,' says Gavin.

"'Na, my mind's made up,' said she.

"'Ye would sune get anither man,' he says, earnestly.

"'Hoo do I ken that?' she speirs, rale sensibly, I thocht, for men's no sae easy to get.

"''Am sure o' 't,' Gavin says, wi' michty conviction in his voice, 'for ye're bonny to look at, an' weel-kent for bein' a guid body.'

"'Ay,' says Mag, 'I'm glad ye like me, Gavin, for ye have to tak me.'"

" That put a clincher on him," interrupted Hendry.

" He was loth to gie in," replied Tammas, "so he says, 'Ye think 'am a fine character, Marget Lownie, but ye're very far mista'en.   I wouldna wonder but what I was lossin' my place some o' thae days, an' syne whaur would ye be ? — Marget

Lownie,' he goes on, ''am nat'rally lazy an' fond o' the drink. As sure as ye stand there, 'am a reglar deevil!'"

"That was strong language," said Hendry, "but he would be wantin' to fleg (frighten) her?"

"Juist so, but he didna manage 't, for Mag says, 'We a' ha'e oor faults, Gavin, an' deevil or no deevil, ye're the man for me!'

"Gavin thocht a bit," continued Tammas, "an' syne he tries her on a new tack. 'Marget Lownie,' he says, 'yer father's an auld man noo, an' he has naebody but yersel to look after him. I'm thinkin' it would be kind o' cruel o' me to tak ye awa frae him?'"

"Mag wouldna be ta'en wi' that; she wasna born on a Sawbath," said Jess, using one of her favourite sayings.

"She wasna," answered Tammas. "Says she, 'Hae nae fear on that score, Gavin; my father's fine willin' to spare me!'"

"An' that ended it?"

"Ay, that ended it."

"Did ye tak it doun in writin'?" asked Hendry.

"There was nae need," said Tammas, handing round his snuff-mull. "No, I never touched paper. When I saw the thing was settled, I left them to their coortin'. They're to tak a look at Snecky Hobart's auld hoose the nicht. It's to let."

CHAPTER XVI

THE SON FROM LONDON

In the spring of the year there used to come to Thrums a painter from nature whom Hendry spoke of as the drawer. He lodged with Jess in my attic, and when the weavers met him they said, "Weel, drawer," and then passed on, grinning. Tammas Haggart was the first to say this.

The drawer was held a poor man because he straggled about the country looking for subjects for his draws, and Jess, as was her way, gave him many comforts for which she would not charge. That, I daresay, was why he painted for her a little portrait of Jamie. When the drawer came back to Thrums he always found the painting in a frame in the room. Here I must make a confession about Jess. She did not in her secret mind think the portrait quite the thing, and as soon as the drawer departed it was removed from the frame to make way for a calendar. The deception was very innocent, Jess being anxious not to hurt the donor's feelings.

To those who have the artist's eye, the picture

which hangs in my school-house now, does not show a handsome lad, Jamie being short and dapper, with straw-coloured hair, and a chin that ran away into his neck. That is how I once regarded him, but I have little heart for criticism of those I like, and, despite his madness for a season, of which, alas, I shall have to tell, I am always Jamie's friend. Even to hear any one disparaging the appearance of Jess's son is to me a pain.

All Jess's acquaintances knew that in the beginning of every month a registered letter reached her from London. To her it was not a matter to keep secret. She was proud that the help she and Hendry needed in the gloaming of their lives should come from her beloved son, and the neighbours esteemed Jamie because he was good to his mother. Jess had more humour than any other woman I have known while Leeby was but sparingly endowed; yet, as the month neared its close, it was the daughter who put on the humorist, Jess thinking money too serious a thing to jest about. Then if Leeby had a moment for gossip, as when ironing a dickey for Hendry, and the iron was a trifle too hot, she would look archly at me before addressing her mother in these words:

"Will he send, think ye?"

Jess, who had a conviction that he would send, affected surprise at the question.

"Will Jamie send this month, do ye mean?

Na, oh, losh no! it's no to be expeckit. Na, he couldna do't this time."

"That's what ye aye say, but he aye sends. Yes, an' vara weel ye ken 'at he will send."

"Na, na, Leeby; dinna let me ever think o' sic a thing this month."

"As if ye wasna thinkin' o't day an' nicht!"

"He's terrible mindfu', Leeby, but he doesna hae't. Na, no this month; mebbe next month."

"Do you mean to tell me, mother, 'at ye'll no be up oot o' yer bed on Monunday an hour afore yer usual time, lookin' for the post?"

"Na, no this time. I may be up, an' tak a look for 'im, but no expeckin' a registerdy; na, na, that wouldna be reasonable."

"Reasonable here, reasonable there, up you'll be, keekin' (peering) through the blind to see if the post's comin', ay, an' what's mair, the post will come, and a registerdy in his hand wi' fifteen shillings in't at the least."

"Dinna say fifteen, Leeby; I would never think o' sic a sum. Mebbe five — "

"Five! I wonder to hear ye. Vera weel you ken 'at since he had twenty-twa shillings in the week he's never sent less than half a sovereign."

"No, but we canna expeck — "

"Expeck! No, but it's no expeck, it's get."

On the Monday morning when I came down-stairs, Jess was in her chair by the window, beaming, a piece of paper in her hand. I did not require to be told about it, but I was told. Jess had been up before Leeby could get the fire lit, with great difficulty reaching the window in her bare feet, and many a time had she said that the post must be by.

"Havers," said Leeby, "he winna be for an hour yet. Come awa' back to your bed."

"Na, he maun be by," Jess would say in a few minutes; "ou, we couldna expeck this month."

So it went on until Jess's hand shook the blind.

"He's comin', Leeby, he's comin'. He'll no hae naething, na, I couldna expeck —— He's by!"

"I dinna believe it," cried Leeby, running to the window, "he's juist at his tricks again."

This was in reference to a way our saturnine post had of pretending that he brought no letters and passing the door. Then he turned back. "Mistress McQumpha," he cried, and whistled.

"Run, Leeby, run," said Jess, excitedly.

Leeby hastened to the door, and came back with a registered letter.

"Registerdy," she cried in triumph, and Jess, with fond hands, opened the letter. By the time I came down the money was hid away in a box beneath the bed, where not even Leeby could find it, and Jess was on her chair hugging the letter. She preserved all her registered envelopes.

THE SON FROM LONDON

This was the first time I had been in Thrums when Jamie was expected for his ten days' holiday, and for a week we discussed little else. Though he had written saying when he would sail for Dundee, there was quite a possibility of his appearing on the brae at any moment, for he liked to take Jess and Leeby by surprise. Hendry there was no surprising, unless he was in the mood for it, and the coolness of him was one of Jess's grievances. Just two years earlier Jamie came north a week before his time, and his father saw him from the window. Instead of crying out in amazement or hacking his face, for he was shaving at the time, Henry calmly wiped his razor on the window-sill, and said —

" Ay, there's Jamie."

Jamie was a little disappointed at being seen in this way, for he had been looking forward for four and forty hours to repeating the sensation of the year before. On that occasion he had got to the door unnoticed, where he stopped to listen. I daresay he checked his breath, the better to catch his mother's voice, for Jess being an invalid, Jamie thought of her first. He had Leeby sworn to write the truth about her, but many an anxious hour he had on hearing that she was "complaining fell (considerably) about her back the day," Leeby, as he knew, being frightened to alarm him. Jamie, too, had given his promise to tell exactly how he was keeping, but often he wrote that he was "fine" when Jess had her doubts. When Hendry wrote he spread himself over the table, and said that Jess was "juist about it," or "aff and on," which does not tell much. So Jamie hearkened painfully at the door, and by and by heard his mother say to Leeby that she was sure the teapot was running out. Perhaps that voice was as sweet to him as the music of a maiden to her lover, but Jamie did not rush into his mother's arms. Jess has told me with a beaming face how craftily he behaved. The old man, of lungs that shook Thrums by night, who went from door to door selling firewood, had a way of shoving doors rudely open and crying —

" Ony rozetty roots ? " and him Jamie imitated.

"Juist think," Jess said, as she recalled the incident, " what a startle we got. As we think, Pete kicks open the door and cries oot, ' Ony rozetty roots ? ' and Leeby says ' No,' and gangs to shut the door. Next minute she screeches, ' What, what, what ! ' and in walks Jamie ! "

Jess was never able to decide whether it was more delightful to be taken aback in this way or to prepare for Jamie. Sudden excitement was bad for her according to Hendry, who got his medical knowledge second-hand from persons under treatment, but with Jamie's appearance on the threshold Jess's health began to improve. This time he kept to the appointed day, and the house was turned

upside down in his honour. Such a polish did
Leeby put on the flagons which hung on the
kitchen wall, that, passing between them and the
window, I thought once I had been struck by
lightning. On the morning of the day that was to
bring him, Leeby was up at two o'clock, and eight
hours before he could possibly arrive Jess had a
night-shirt warming for him at the fire. I was no
longer anybody, except as a person who could give
Jamie advice. Jess told me what I was to say.
The only thing he and his mother quarrelled about
was the underclothing she would swaddle him in,
and Jess asked me to back her up in her entreaties.

"There's no a doubt," she said, "but what it's
a hantle caulder here than in London, an' it would
be a terrible business if he was to tak the cauld."

Jamie was to sail from London to Dundee, and
come on to Thrums from Tilliedrum in the post-
cart. The road at that time, however, avoided
the brae, and at a certain point Jamie's custom was
to alight, and take the short cut home, along a
farm road and up the commonty. Here, too,
Hookey Crewe, the post, deposited his passenger's
box, which Hendry wheeled home in a barrow.
Long before the cart had lost sight of Tilliedrum,
Jess was at her window.

"Tell her Hookey's often late on Monundays,"
Leeby whispered to me, "for she'll gang oot o'
her mind if she thinks there's onything wrang."

Soon Jess was painfully excited, though she sat as still as salt.

"It maun be yer time," she said, looking at both Leeby and me, for in Thrums we went out and met our friends.

"Hoots," retorted Leeby, trying to be hardy, "Hookey canna be oot o' Tilliedrum yet."

"He maun hae startit lang syne."

"I wonder at ye, mother, puttin' yersel in sic a state. Ye'll be ill when he comes."

"Na, am no in nae state, Leeby, but there'll no be nae accident, will there?"

"It's most provokin' 'at ye will think 'at every time Jamie steps into a machine there'll be an accident. Am sure if ye would tak mair after my father, it would be a blessin'. Look hoo cool he is."

"Whaur is he, Leeby?"

"Oh, I dinna ken. The henmost time I saw him he was layin' doon the law aboot something to T'nowhead."

"It's an awfu' wy that he has o' ga'en oot withoot a word. I wouldna wonder 'at he's no bein' in time to meet Jamie, an' that would be a pretty business."

"Od, ye're sure he'll be in braw time."

"But he hasna ta'en the barrow wi' him, an' hoo is Jamie's luggage to be brocht up withoot a barrow?"

" Barrow! He took the barrow to the saw-mill an hour syne to pick it up at Rob Angus's on the wy."

Several times Jess was sure she saw the cart in the distance, and implored us to be off.

" I'll tak no settle till ye're awa," she said, her face now flushed and her hands working nervously.

" We've time to gang and come twa or three times yet," remonstrated Leeby; but Jess gave me so beseeching a look that I put on my hat. Then Hendry dandered in to change his coat deliberately, and when the three of us set off, we left Jess with her eye on the door by which Jamie must enter. He was her only son now, and she had not seen him for a year.

On the way down the commonty, Leeby had the honour of being twice addressed as Miss Mc-Qumpha, but her father was Hendry to all, which shows that we make our social position for ourselves. Hendry looked forward to Jamie's annual appearance only a little less hungrily than Jess, but his pulse still beat regularly. Leeby would have considered it almost wicked to talk of anything except Jamie now, but Hendry cried out comments on the tatties, yesterday's roup, the fall in jute, to everybody he encountered. When he and a crony had their say and parted, it was their custom to continue the conversation in shouts until they were out of hearing.

Only to Jess at her window was the cart late that afternoon. Jamie jumped from it in the long great-coat that had been new to Thrums the year before, and Hendry said calmly —

"Ay, Jamie."

Leeby and Jamie made signs that they recognized each other as brother and sister, but I was the only one with whom he shook hands. He was smart in his movements and quite the gentleman, but the Thrums ways took hold of him again at once. He even inquired for his mother in a tone that was meant to deceive me into thinking he did not care how she was.

Hendry would have had a talk out of him on the spot, but was reminded of the luggage. We took the heavy farm road, and soon we were at the saw-mill. I am naturally leisurely, but we climbed the commonty at a stride. Jamie pretended to be calm, but in a dark place I saw him take Leeby's hand, and after that he said not a word. His eyes were fixed on the elbow of the brae, where he would come into sight of his mother's window. Many, many a time, I know, that lad had prayed to God for still another sight of the window with his mother at it. So we came to the corner where the stile is that Sam'l Dickie jumped in the race for T'nowhead's Bell, and before Jamie was the house of his childhood and his mother's window, and the fond, anxious face of his mother herself. My eyes are dull, and I did not see her, but suddenly Jamie cried out, "My mother!" and Leeby and I were left behind. When I reached the kitchen Jess was crying, and her son's arms were round her neck. I went away to my attic.

There was only one other memorable event of that day. Jamie had finished his tea, and we all sat round him, listening to his adventures and opinions. He told us how the country should be governed, too, and perhaps put on airs a little. Hendry asked the questions, and Jamie answered them as pat as if he and his father were going through the Shorter Catechism. When Jamie told anything marvellous, as how many towels were used at the shop in a day, or that twopence was the charge for a single shave, his father screwed his mouth together as if preparing to whistle, and then instead made a curious clucking noise with his tongue, which was reserved for the expression of absolute amazement. As for Jess, who was given to making much of me, she ignored my remarks and laughed hilariously at jokes of Jamie's which had been received in silence from me a few minutes before.

Slowly it came to me that Leeby had something on her mind, and that Jamie was talking to her with his eyes. I learned afterwards that they were plotting how to get me out of the kitchen, but were too impatient to wait. Thus it was that the great event happened in my presence. Jamie rose and stood near Jess — I daresay he had planned the scene frequently. Then he produced from his pocket a purse, and coolly opened it. Silence fell upon us as we saw that purse. From it he took a neatly-folded piece of paper, crumpled it into a ball, and flung it into Jess's lap.

I cannot say whether Jess knew what it was. Her hand shook, and for a moment she let the ball of paper lie there.

"Open't up," cried Leeby, who was in the secret.

"What 's't?" asked Hendry, drawing nearer.

"It's juist a bit paper Jamie flung at me," said Jess, and then she unfolded it.

"It's a five-pound note!" cried Hendry.

"Na, na, oh keep us, no," said Jess; but she knew it was.

For a time she could not speak.

"I canna tak it, Jamie," she faltered at last.

But Jamie waved his hand, meaning that it was nothing, and then, lest he should burst, hurried out into the garden, where he walked up and down whistling. May God bless the lad, thought I. I do not know the history of that five-pound note, but well aware I am that it grew slowly out of pence and silver, and that Jamie denied his passions many things for this great hour. His sacrifices watered his young heart and kept it fresh and tender. Let us no longer cheat our consciences by talking of filthy lucre. Money may always be a beautiful thing. It is we who make it grimy.

CHAPTER XVII

A HOME FOR GENIUSES

FROM hints he had let drop at odd times I knew that Tammas Haggart had a scheme for geniuses, but not until the evening after Jamie's arrival did I get it out of him. Hendry was with Jamie at the fishing, and it came about that Tammas and I had the pig-sty to ourselves.

" Of course," he said, when we had got a grip of the subject, " I dount pretend as my ideas is to be followed withoot deeviation, but ondootedly something should be done for geniuses, them bein' aboot the only class as we do naething for. Yet they're fowk to be prood o', an' we shouldna let them overdo the thing, nor run into debt; na, na. There was Robbie Burns, noo, as real a genius as ever — "

At the pig-sty, where we liked to have more than one topic, we had frequently to tempt Tammas away from Burns.

" Your scheme," I interposed, " is for living geniuses, of course ? "

" Ay," he said, thoughtfully, " them 'at's gone

canna be brocht back. Weel, my idea is 'at a
Home should be built for geniuses at the public
expense, whaur they could all live thegither, an
be decently looked after. Na, no in London;
that's no my plan, but I would hae't within an
hour's distance o' London, say five mile frae the
market-place, an' standin' in a bit garden, whaur
the geniuses could walk aboot arm-in-arm, com-
posin' their minds."

"You would have the grounds walled in, I suppose, so that the public could not intrude?"

"Weel, there's a difficulty there, because, ye'll
observe, as the public would support the insti-
tootion, they would hae a kind o' richt to look in.
How-some-ever, I daur say we could arrange to
fling the grounds open to the public once a week
on condition 'at they didna speak to the geniuses.
I'm thinkin' 'at if there was a small chairge for
admission the Home could be made self-supportin'.
Losh! to think 'at if there had been sic an insti-
tootion in his time a man micht hae sat on the bit
dyke and watched Robbie Burns danderin' roond
the—"

"You would divide the Home into suites of
rooms, so that every inmate would have his own
apartments?"

"Not by no means; na, na. The mair I read
aboot geniuses the mair clearly I see as their wy
o' living alane ower muckle is ane o' the things as

breaks doon their health, and makes them meeserable. I' the Home they would hae a bedroom
apiece, but the parlour an' the other sittin'-rooms
would be for all, so as they could enjoy ane another's company. The management? Oh, that's
aisy. The superintendent would be a medical
man appointed by Parliament, and he would hae
men-servants to do his biddin'."

"Not all men-servants, surely?"

"Every one o' them. Man, geniuses is no to be
trusted wi' womenfolk. No, even Robbie Bu—"

"So he did; but would the inmates have to put
themselves entirely in the superintendent's hands?"

"Nae doubt; an' they would see it was the wisest
thing they could do. He would be careful o' their
health, an' send them early to bed as weel as hae
them up at eight sharp. Geniuses' healths is
always breakin' doon because of late hours, as in
the case o' the lad wha used often to begin his immortal writin's at twal o'clock at nicht, a thing 'at
would ruin ony constitootion. But the superintendent would see as they had a tasty supper at
nine o'clock — something as agreed wi' them.
Then for half an hour they would quiet their brains
readin' oot aloud, time about, frae sic a book as
the 'Pilgrim's Progress,' an' the gas would be
turned aff at ten precisely."

"When would you have them up in the morning?"

"At sax in summer an' seven in winter. The superintendent would see as they were all properly bathed every mornin', cleanliness bein' most important for the preservation o' health."

"This sounds well; but suppose a genius broke the rules—lay in bed, for instance, reading by the light of a candle after hours, or refused to take his bath in the morning?"

"The superintendent would hae to punish him. The genius would be sent back to his bed, maybe. An' if he lay lang i' the mornin' he would hae to gang withoot his breakfast."

"That would be all very well where the inmate only broke the regulations once in a way; but suppose he were to refuse to take his bath day after day (and, you know, geniuses are said to be eccentric in that particular), what would be done? You could not starve him; geniuses are too scarce."

"Na, na; in a case like that he would hae to be reported to the public. The thing would hae to come afore the Hoose of Commons. Ay, the superintendent would get a member o' the Opposeetion to ask a queistion such as 'Can the honourable gentleman, the Secretary of State for Home Affairs, inform the Hoose whether it is a fac that Mr. Sic-a-one, the well-known genius, at present resident in the Home for Geniuses, has, contrairy to regulations, perseestently and obstinately refused to change his linen; and, if so, whether the **Government** proposes to take ony steps in the matter?' The newspapers would report the discussion next mornin', an' so it would be made public withoot onnecessary ootlay."

"In a general way, however, you would give the geniuses perfect freedom? They could work when they liked, and come and go when they liked?"

"Not so. The superintendent would fix the hours o' wark, an' they would all write, or whatever it was, thegither in one large room. Man, man, it would mak a grand draw for a painter-chield, that room, wi' all the geniuses working awa' thegither."

"But when the labors of the day were over the genius would be at liberty to make calls by himself or to run up, say, to London for an hour or two?"

"Hoots no, that would spoil everything. It's the drink, ye see, as does for a terrible lot o' geniuses. Even Rob—"

"Alas! yes. But would you have them all teetotalers?"

"What do ye tak me for? Na, na; the superintendent would allow them one glass o' toddy every nicht, an' mix it himsel; but he would never get the keys o' the press, whaur he kept the drink, oot o' his hands. They would never be allowed oot o' the gairden either, withoot a man to look after them; an' I wouldna burthen them wi' ower muckle pocket-money. Saxpence in the week would be suffeecient."

"How about their clothes?"

"They would get twa suits a year, wi' the letter G sewed on the shoulders, so as if they were lost they could be recognized and brocht back."

"Certainly it is a scheme deserving considera-tion, and I have no doubt our geniuses would jump at it; but you must remember that some of them would have wives."

"Ay, an' some o' them would hae husbands. I've been thinkin' that oot, an' I daur say the best plan would be to partition aff a pairt o' the Home for female geniuses."

"Would Parliament elect the members?"

"I wouldna trust them. The election would hae to be by competitive examination. Na, I canna say wha would draw up the queistions. The scheme's juist growin' i' my mind, but the mair I think o't the better I like it."

CHAPTER XVIII

LEEBY AND JAMIE

By the bank of the Quharity on a summer day I have seen a barefooted girl gaze at the running water until tears filled her eyes. That was the birth of romance. Whether this love be but a beautiful dream I cannot say, but this we see, that it comes to all, and colours the whole future life with gold. Leeby must have dreamt it, but I did not know her then. I have heard of a man who would have taken her far away into a county where the corn is yellow when it is still green with us, but she would not leave her mother, nor was it him she saw in her dream. From her earliest days, when she was still a child staggering round the garden with Jamie in her arms, her duty lay before her, straight as the burying-ground road. Jess had need of her in the little home at the top of the brae, where God, looking down upon her as she scrubbed and gossipped and sat up all night with her ailing mother, and never missed the prayer-meeting, and adored the minister, did not perhaps think her the least of His handmaids. Her years were less than thirty when He took her away, but she had few days that were altogether dark. Those who bring sunshine to the lives of others cannot keep it from themselves.

The love Leeby bore for Jamie was such that in their younger days it shamed him. Other laddies knew of it, and flung it at him until he dared Leeby to let on in public that he and she were related.

"Hoo is your lass?" they used to cry to him, inventing a new game.

"I saw Leeby lookin' for ye," they would say; "she's wearyin' for ye to gang an' play wi' her."

Then if they were not much bigger boys than himself, Jamie got them against the dyke and hit them hard until they publicly owned to knowing that she was his sister, and that he was not fond of her.

"It distressed him mair than ye could believe, though," Jess has told me; "an' when he came hame he would greet an' say 'at Leeby disgraced him."

Leeby, of course, suffered for her too obvious affection.

"I wonder 'at ye dinna try to control yersel," Jamie would say to her, as he grew bigger.

"Am sure," said Leeby, "I never gie ye a look if there's onybody there."

"A look! You're ay lookin' at me sae fond-like 'at I dinna ken what wy to turn."

137

"Weel, I canna help it," said Leeby, probably beginning to whimper.

If Jamie was in a very bad temper he left her, after this, to her own reflections; but he was naturally soft-hearted.

"Am no tellin' ye no to care for me," he told her, "but juist to keep it mair to yersel. Naebody would ken frae me 'at am fond o' ye."

"Mebbe yer no?" said Leeby.

"Ay, am I, but I can keep it secret. When we're in the hoose am juist richt fond o' ye."

"Do ye love me, Jamie?"

Jamie waggled his head in irritation.

"Love," he said, "is an awful like word to use when fowk's weel. Ye shouldna speir sic annoyin' queistions."

"But if ye juist say ye love me I'll never let on again afore fowk 'at yer onything to me ava."

"Ay, ye often say that."

"Do ye no believe my word?"

"I believe fine ye mean what ye say, but ye forget yersel when the time comes."

"Juist try me this time."

"Weel, then, I do."

"Do what?" asked the greedy Leeby.

"What ye said."

"I said love."

"Well," said Jamie, "I do't."

"What do ye do? Say the word."

"Na," said Jamie, "I winna say the word. It's no a word to say, but I do't."

That was all she could get out of him, unless he was stricken with remorse, when he even went the length of saying the word.

"Leeby kent perfectly weel," Jess has said, "'at it was a trial to Jamie to tak her ony gait, an' I often used to say to her 'at I wondered at her want o' pride in priggin' wi' him. Ay, but if she could juist get a promise wrung oot o' him, she didna care hoo muckle she had to prig. Syne they quarrelled, an' ane or baith o' them grat (cried) afore they made it up. I mind when Jamie went to the fishin' Leeby was aye terrible keen to get wi' him, but ye see he wouldna be seen gaen through the toon wi' her. 'If ye let me gang,' she said to him, 'I'll no seek to go through the toon wi' ye. Na, I'll gang roond by the Roods an' you can tak the buryin'-ground road, so as we can meet on the hill.' Yes, Leeby was willin' to agree wi' a' that, juist to get gaen wi' him. I've seen lassies makkin' themsels sma' for lads often enough, but I never saw ane 'at prigged so muckle wi' her ain brother. Na, it's other lassies' brothers they like as a rule."

"But though Jamie was terrible reserved aboot it," said Leeby, "he was as fond o' me as ever I was o' him. Ye mind the time I had the measles, mother?"

"Am no likely to forget it, Leeby," said Jess, "an' you blind wi' them for three days. Ay, ay, Jamie was richt taen up aboot ye. I mind he broke open his pirly (money-box), an' bocht a ha'penny worth o' something to ye every day."

"An' ye hinna forgotten the stick?"

"'Deed no, I hinna. Ye see," Jess explained to me, "Leeby was lyin' ben the hoose, an' Jamie wasna allowed to gang near her for fear o' infection. Weel, he gat a lang stick—it was a pea-stick—an' put it aneath the door an' waggled it. Ay, he did that a curran times every day, juist to let her see he was thinkin' o' her."

"Mair than that," said Leeby, "he cried oot 'at he loved me."

"Ay, but juist aince," Jess said, "I dinna mind o't but aince. It was the time the doctor came late, an' Jamie, being waukened by him, thocht ye was deein'. I mind as if it was yesterday hoo he cam runnin' to the door an' cried oot, 'I do love ye, Leeby; I love ye richt.' The doctor got a start when he heard the voice, but he laughed loud when he un'erstood."

"He had nae business, though," said Leeby, "to tell onybody."

"He was a rale clever man, the doctor," Jess explained to me, "ay, he kent me as weel as though he'd gaen through me wi' a lichted candle. It got oot through him, an' the young billies took to sayin' to Jamie, 'Ye do love her, Jamie; ay, ye love her richt.' The only reglar fecht I ever kent Jamie hae was wi' a lad 'at cried that to him. It was Bowlegs Chirsty's laddie. Ay, but when she got better Jamie blamed Leeby."

"He no only blamed me," said Leeby, "but he wanted me to pay him back a' the bawbees he had spent on me."

"Ay, an' I sepad he got them too," said Jess.

In time Jamie became a barber in Tilliedrum, trudging many heavy miles there and back twice a day that he might sleep at home, trudging bravely I was to say, but it was what he was born to, and there was hardly an alternative. This was the time I saw most of him, and he and Leeby were often in my thoughts. There is as terrible a bubble in the little kettle as on the cauldron of the world, and some of the scenes between Jamie and Leeby were great tragedies, comedies, what you will, until the kettle was taken off the fire. Hers was the more placid temper; indeed, only in one way could Jamie suddenly rouse her to fury. That was when he hinted that she had a large number of frocks. Leeby knew that there could never be more than a Sabbath frock and an everyday gown for her, both of her mother's making, but Jamie's insinuations were more than she could bear. Then I have seen her seize and shake him. I know from Jess that Leeby cried herself hoarse the day Joey was buried, because her little black frock was not ready for wear.

Until he went to Tilliedrum Jamie had been more a stay-at-home boy than most. The warmth of Jess's love had something to do with keeping his heart aglow, but more, I think, he owed to Leeby. Tilliedrum was his introduction to the world, and for a little it took his head. I was in the house the Sabbath day that he refused to go to church.

He went out in the forenoon to meet the Tilliedrum lads, who were to take him off for a holiday in a cart. Hendry was more wrathful than I remember ever to have seen him, though I have heard how he did with the lodger who broke the Lord's Day. This lodger was a tourist who thought, in folly surely rather than in hardness of heart, to test the religious convictions of an Auld Licht by insisting on paying his bill on a Sabbath morning. He offered the money to Jess, with the warning that if she did not take it now she might never see it. Jess was so kind and good to her lodgers that he could not have known her long who troubled her with this poor trick. She was sorely in need at the time, and entreated the thoughtless man to have some pity on her.

"Now or never," he said, holding out the money.

"Put it on the dresser," said Jess at last, "an' I'll get it the morn."

The few shillings were laid on the dresser, where they remained unfingered until Hendry, with Leeby and Jamie, came in from church.

" What siller's that ? " asked Hendry, and then Jess confessed what she had done.

" I wonder at ye, woman," said Hendry, sternly; and lifting the money he climbed up to the attic with it.

He pushed open the door, and confronted the lodger.

" Take back yer siller," he said laying it on the table, " an' leave my hoose. Man, you're a pitiable crittur to tak the chance, when I was oot, o' playin' upon the poverty o' an onweel woman."

It was with such unwonted severity as this that Hendry called upon Jamie to follow him to church; but the boy went off, and did not return till dusk, defiant and miserable. Jess had been so terrified that she forgave him everything for sight of his face, and Hendry prayed for him at family worship with too much unction. But Leeby cried as if her tender heart would break. For a long time Jamie refused to look at her, but at last he broke down.

" If ye go on like that," he said, " I'll gang awa oot an' droon mysel, or be a sojer."

This was no uncommon threat of his, and sometimes, when he went off, banging the door violently, she ran after him and brought him back. This time she only wept the more, and so both went to bed in misery. It was after midnight that Jamie rose and crept to Leeby's bedside. Leeby was shaking the bed in her agony. Jess heard what they said.

"Leeby," said Jamie, "dinna greet, an' I'll never do't again."

He put his arms round her, and she kissed him passionately.

"O, Jamie," she said, "hae ye prayed to God to forgie ye?"

Jamie did not speak.

"If ye was to die this nicht," cried Leeby, "an' you no made it up wi' God, ye wouldna gang to heaven. Jamie, I canna sleep till ye've made it up wi' God."

But Jamie still hung back. Leeby slipped from her bed, and went down on her knees.

"O God, O dear God," she cried, "mak Jamie to pray to you!"

Then Jamie went down on his knees too, and they made it up with God together.

This is a little thing for me to remember all these years, and yet how fresh and sweet it keeps Leeby in my memory.

Away up in the glen, my lonely schoolhouse lying deep, as one might say, in a sea of snow, I had many hours in the years long by for thinking of my friends in Thrums and mapping out the future of Leeby and Jamie. I saw Hendry and

Jess taken to the churchyard, and Leeby left alone in the house. I saw Jamie fulfil his promise to his mother, and take Leeby, that stainless young woman, far away to London, where they had a home together. Ah, but these were only the idle dreams of a dominie. The Lord willed it otherwise.

CHAPTER XIX

A TALE OF A GLOVE

So long as Jamie was not the lad, Jess twinkled gleefully over tales of sweethearting. There was little Kitty Lamby who used to skip in of an evening, and, squatting on a stool near the window, unwind the roll of her enormities. A wheedling thing she was, with an ambition to drive men crazy, but my presence killed the gossip on her tongue, though I liked to look at her. When I entered, the wag at the wa' clock had again possession of the kitchen. I never heard more than the end of a sentence:

"An' did he really say he would fling himsel into the dam, Kitty?"

Or — "True as death, Jess, he kissed me."

Then I wandered away from the kitchen, where I was not wanted, and marvelled to know that Jess of the tender heart laughed most merrily when he really did say that he was going straight to the dam. As no body was found in the dam in those days, whoever he was he must have thought better of it.

But let Kitty, or any other maid, cast a glinting eye on Jamie, then Jess no longer smiled. If he returned the glance she sat silent in her chair till Leeby laughed away her fears.

"Jamie's no the kind, mother," Leeby would say. "Na, he's quiet, but he sees through them. They dinna draw his leg (get over him)."

"Ye never can tell, Leeby. The laddies 'at's maist ill to get sometimes gangs up in a flame a' at aince, like a bit o' paper."

"Ay, weel, at ony rate Jamie's no on fire yet."

Though clever beyond her neighbours, Jess lost all her sharpness if they spoke of a lassie for Jamie.

"I warrant," Tibbie Birse said one day in my hearing, "'at there's some leddie in London he's thinkin' o'. Ay, he's been a guid laddie to ye, but i' the course o' nature he'll be settlin' dune soon."

Jess did not answer, but she was a picture of woe.

"Ye're lettin' what Tibbie Birse said lie on yer mind," Leeby remarked, when Tibbie was gone. "What can it maiter what she thinks?"

"I canna help it, Leeby," said Jess. "Na, an' I canna bear to think o' Jamie bein' mairit. It would lay me low to loss my laddie. No yet, no yet."

"But, mother," said Leeby, quoting from the minister at weddings, "ye wouldna be lossin' a son, but juist gainin' a dochter."

"Dinna haver, Leeby," answered Jess, "I want nane o' thae dochters; na, na."

This talk took place while we were still awaiting Jamie's coming. He had only been with us one day when Jess made a terrible discovery. She was looking so mournful when I saw her, that I asked Leeby what was wrong.

"She's brocht it on hersel," said Leeby. "Ye see she was up sune i' the mornin' to begin to the darnin' o' Jamie's stockins an' to warm his sark at the fire afore he put it on. He woke up, an' cried to her 'at he wasna accustomed to hae'n his things warmed for him. Ay, he cried it oot fell thrawn, so she took it into her head 'at there was something in his pouch he didna want her to see. She was even onaisy last nicht."

I asked what had aroused Jess's suspicions last night.

"Ou, ye would notice 'at she sat devourin' him wi' her een, she was so lifted up at hae'n 'im again. Weel, she says noo 'at she saw 'im twa or three times put his hand in his pouch as if he was findin' to mak sure 'at something was safe. So when he fell asleep again this mornin' she got haud o' his jacket to see if there was onything in't. I advised her no to do't, but she couldna help herself. She put in her hand, an' pu'd it oot. That's what's makkin' her look sae ill."

"But what was it she found?"

" Did I no tell ye? I'm ga'en dottle, I think.
It was a glove, a woman's glove, in a bit paper.
Ay, though she's sittin' still she's near frantic."

I said I supposed Jess had put the glove back
in Jamie's pocket.

" Na," said Leeby, " 'deed no. She wanted to
fling it on the back o' the fire, but I wouldna let
her. That's it she has aneath her apron."

Later in the day I remarked to Leeby that Jamie
was very dull.

" He's missed it," she explained.

" Has any one mentioned it to him," I asked,
" or has he inquired about it?"

" Na," said Leeby, " there hasna been a syllup
(syllable) aboot it. My mother's fleid to mention't,
an' he doesna like to speak aboot it either."

" Perhaps he thinks he has lost it?"

" Nae fear o' him," Leeby said. " Na, he kens
fine wha has't."

I never knew how Jamie came by the glove,
nor whether it had originally belonged to her who
made him forget the window at the top of the brae.
At the time I looked on as at play-acting, rejoicing
in the happy ending. Alas! in the real life how
are we to know when we have reached an end?

But this glove, I say, may not have been that
woman's, and if it was, she had not then bedevilled
him. He was too sheepish to demand it back
from his mother, and already he cared for it too

much to laugh at Jess's theft with Leeby. So it was that a curious game at chess was played with the glove, the players a silent pair.

Jamie cared little to read books, but on the day following Jess's discovery, I found him on his knees in the attic, looking through mine. A little box, without a lid, held them all, but they seemed a great library to him.

"There's readin' for a lifetime in them," he said. "I was juist takkin' a look through them."

His face was guilty, however, as if his hand had been caught in a money-bag, and I wondered what had enticed the lad to my books. I was still standing pondering when Leeby ran up the stair; she was so active that she generally ran, and she grudged the time lost in recovering her breath.

"I'll put yer books richt," she said, making her word good as she spoke. "I kent Jamie had been ransackin' up here, though he came up rale canny. Ay, ye would notice he was in his stockin' soles."

I had not noticed this, but I remembered now his slipping from the room very softly. If he wanted a book, I told Leeby, he could have got it without any display of cunning.

"It's no a book he's lookin' for," she said, "na, it's his glove."

The time of day was early for Leeby to gossip, but I detained her for a moment.

"My mother's hodded (hid) it," she explained,

"an he winna speir nae queistions. But he's lookin' for't. He was ben in the room searchin' the drawers when I was up i' the toon in the forenoon. Ye see he pretends no to be carin' afore me, an' though my mother's sittin' sae quiet-like at the window she's hearkenin' a' the time. Ay, an' he thocht I had hod it up here."

But where, I asked, was the glove hid.

"I ken nae mair than yersel," said Leeby. "My mother's gien to hoddin' things. She has a place aneath the bed whaur she keeps the siller, an' she's no speakin' aboot the glove to me noo, because she thinks Jamie an' me's in comp (company). I speired at her whaur she had hod it, but she juist said, 'What would I be doin' hoddin't?' She'll never admit to me 'at she hods the siller either."

Next day Leeby came to me with the latest news.

"He's found it," she said, "ay, he's got the glove again. Ye see what put him on the wrang scent was a notion 'at I had put it some gait. He kent 'at if she'd hod it, the kitchen maun be the place, but he thocht she'd gi'en it to me to hod. He came upon't by accident. It was aneath the paddin' o' her chair."

Here, I thought, was the end of the glove incident, but I was mistaken. There were no presses or drawers with locks in the house, and Jess got hold of the glove again. I suppose she had reasoned out no line of action. She merely hated the thought that Jamie should have a woman's glove in his possession.

"She beats a' wi' 'cuteness," Leeby said to me. "Jamie didna put the glove back in his pouch. Na, he kens her ower weel by this time. She was up, though, lang afore he was wauken, an' she gaed almost strecht to the place whaur he had hod it. I believe she lay waukin a' nicht thinkin' oot whaur it would be. Ay, it was aneath the mattress. I saw her hodden't i' the back o' the drawer, but I didna let on."

I quite believed Leeby when she told me afterwards that she had watched Jamie feeling beneath the mattress.

"He had a face," she said, "I assure ye, he had a face, when he discovered the glove was gone again."

"He maun be terrible ta'en up aboot it," Jess said to Leeby, "or he wouldna keep it aneath the mattress."

"Od," said Leeby, "it was yersel 'at drove him to't."

Again Jamie recovered his property, and again Jess got hold of it. This time he looked in vain. I learnt the fate of the glove from Leeby.

"Ye mind 'at she keepit him at hame frae the kirk on Sabbath, because he had a cauld?" Leeby said. "Ay, me or my father would hae a

gey ill cauld afore she would let's bide at hame
frae the kirk; but Jamie's different. Weel, mair
than ance she's been near speakin' to 'im aboot
the glove, but she grew fleid aye. She was so terrified there was something in't.

"On Sabbath, though, she had him to hersel, an'
he wasna so bright as usual. She sat wi' the Bible
on her lap, pretendin' to read, but a' the time she
was takkin' keeks (glances) at him. I dinna ken
'at he was broodin' ower the glove, but she thocht
he was, an' just afore the kirk came oot she
couldna stand it nae langer. She put her hand
in her pouch, an pu'd oot the glove, wi' the paper
round it, just as it had been when she came
upon't.

"'That's yours, Jamie,' she said; 'it was ill-dune
o' me to tak it, but I couldna help it.'

"Jamie put oot his hand, an' syne he drew't
back. 'It's no a thing o' nae consequence, mother,
he said.

"'Wha is she, Jamie?' my mother said.

"He turned awa his heid — so she telt me. 'It's
a lassie in London,' he said, 'I dinna ken her
muckle.'

"'Ye maun ken her weel,' my mother persisted,
'to be carryin' aboot her glove; I'm dootin' ye're
gey fond o' her, Jamie?'

"'Na,' said Jamie, 'am no. There's no naebody
I care for like yersel, mother.'

"'Ye wouldna carry aboot onything o' mine, Jamie,' my mother said; but he says, 'Oh, mother, I carry aboot yer face wi' me aye; an' sometimes at nicht I kind o' greet to think o' ye.'

"Ay, after that I've nae doot he was sittin' wi' his airms aboot her. She didna tell me that, but weel he kens it's what she likes, an' she maks nae pretence o' its no bein'. But for a' he said an' did, she noticed him put the glove back in his inside pouch.

"'It's wrang o' me, Jamie,' she said, 'but I canna bear to think o' ye carryin' that aboot sae carefu'. No, I canna help it.'

"Weel, Jamie, the crittur, took it oot o' his pouch an' kind o' hesitated. Syne he lays't on the back o' the fire, an' they sat thegither glowerin' at it.

"'Noo, mother,' he says, 'you're satisfied, are ye no?'

"Ay," Leeby ended her story, "she said she was satisfied. But she saw 'at he laid it on the fire fell fond-like."

CHAPTER XX

THE LAST NIGHT

"Juist another sax nichts, Jamie," Jess would say, sadly. "Juist fower nichts noo, an' you'll be awa." Even as she spoke seemed to come the last night.

The last night! Reserve slipped unheeded to the floor. Hendry wandered ben and but the house, and Jamie sat at the window holding his mother's hand. You must walk softly now if you would cross that humble threshold. I stop at the door. Then, as now, I was a lonely man, and when the last night came the attic was the place for me.

This family affection, how good and beautiful it is. Men and maids love, and after many years they may rise to this. It is the grand proof of the goodness in human nature, for it means that the more we see of each other the more we find that is lovable. If you would cease to dislike a man, try to get nearer his heart.

Leeby had no longer any excuse for bustling about. Everything was ready — too soon. Hendry had been to the fish-cadger in the square to get a bervie for Jamie's supper, and Jamie had eaten it, trying to look as if it made him happier. His little box was packed and strapped, and stood terribly conspicuous against the dresser. Jess had packed it herself.

"Ye mauna trachle (trouble) yersel, mother," Jamie said, when she had the empty box pulled toward her.

Leeby was wiser.

"Let her do't," she whispered, "it'll keep her frae broodin'."

Jess tied ends of yarn round the stockings to keep them in a little bundle by themselves. So she did with all the other articles.

"No 'at it's ony great affair," she said, for on the last night they were all thirsting to do something for Jamie that would be a great affair to him.

"Ah, ye would wonder, mother," Jamie said, "when I open my box an' find a'thing tied up wi' strings sae careful, it a' comes back to me wi' a rush wha did it, an' am as fond o' thae strings as though they were a grand present. There's the pocky (bag) ye gae mi to keep sewin' things in. I get the wifie I lodge wi' to sew to me, but often when I come upon the pocky I sit an' look at it."

Two chairs were backed to the fire, with under-clothing hanging upside down on them. From the string over the fireplace dangled two pairs of much-darned stockings.

"Ye'll put on baith thae pair o' stockin's, Jamie," said Jess, "juist to please me?"

When he arrived he had rebelled against the extra clothing.

"Ay, will I, mother?" he said now.

Jess put her hand fondly through his ugly hair. How handsome she thought him.

"Ye have a fine brow, Jamie," she said. "I mind the day ye was born sayin' to mysel 'at ye had a fine brow."

"But ye thocht he was to be a lassie, mother," said Leeby.

"Na, Leeby, I didna. I kept sayin' I thocht he would be a lassie because I was fleid he would be; but a' the time I had a presentiment he would be a laddie. It was wi' Joey deein' sae sudden, an' I took on sae terrible aboot 'im 'at I thocht all alang the Lord would gie me another laddie."

"Ay, I wanted 'im to be a laddie mysel," said Hendry, "so as he could tak Joey's place."

Jess's head jerked back involuntarily, and Jamie may have felt her hand shake, for he said in a voice out of Hendry's hearing—

"I never took Joey's place wi' ye, mother."

Jess pressed his hand tightly in her two worn palms, but she did not speak.

"Jamie was richt like Joey when he was a bairn," Hendry said.

Again Jess's head moved, but still she was silent.

"They were sae like," continued Hendry, "'at often I called Jamie by Joey's name."

Jess looked at her husband, and her mouth opened and shut.

"I canna mind 'at you ever did that?" Hendry said.

She shook her head,

"Na," said Hendry, "you never mixed them up. I dinna think ye ever missed Joey sae sair as I did."

Leeby went ben, and stood in the room in the dark; Jamie knew why.

"I'll just gang ben an' speak to Leeby for a meenute," he said to his mother; "I'll no be lang."

"Ay, do that, Jamie," said Jess. "What Leeby's been to me nae tongue can tell. Ye canna bear to hear me speak, I ken, o' the time when Hendry an' me'll be awa, but, Jamie, when that time comes ye'll no forget Leeby?"

"I winna, mother, I winna," said Jamie. "There'll never be a roof ower me 'at's no hers too."

He went ben and shut the door. I do not know what he and Leeby said. Many a time since their earliest youth had these two been closeted together, often to make up their little quarrels in each other's arms. They remained a long time in the room, the shabby room of which Jess and Leeby were so proud, and whatever might be their fears about their mother, they were not anxious for themselves.

Leeby was feeling lusty and well, and she could not know that Jamie required to be reminded of his duty to the folk at home. Jamie would have laughed at the notion. Yet that woman in London must have been waiting for him even then. Leeby, who was about to die, and Jamie, who was to forget his mother, came back to the kitchen with a happy light on their faces. I have with me still the look of love they gave each other before Jamie crossed over to Jess.

"Ye'll gang answer, noo, mother," Leeby said, meaning that it was Jess's bed-time.

"No yet, Leeby," Jess answered, "I'll sit up till the readin's ower."

"I think ye should gang, mother," Jamie said, "an' I'll come an' sit aside ye after ye're i' yer bed."

"Ay, Jamie, I'll no hae ye to sit aside me the morn's nicht, an' hap (cover) me wi' the claes."

"But ye'll gang suner to yer bed, mother."

"I may gang, but I winna sleep. I'll aye be thinkin' o' ye tossin' on the sea. I pray for ye a lang time ilka nicht, Jamie."

"Ay, I ken."

"An' I pictur ye ilka hour o' the day. Ye never gang hame through thae terrible streets at nicht but I'm thinkin' o' ye."

"I would try no to be sae sad, mother," said Leeby. "We've ha'en a richt fine time, have we no?"

"It's been an awfu' happy time," said Jess. "We've ha'en a pleasantness in oor lives 'at comes to few. I ken naebody 'at's ha'en sae muckle happiness one wy or another."

"It's because ye're sae guid, mother," said Jamie.

"Na, Jamie, am no guid ava. It's because my fowk's been sae guid, you an' Hendry an' Leeby an' Joey when he was livin'. I've got a lot mair than my deserts."

"We'll juist look to meetin' next year again, mother. To think o' that keeps me up a' the winter."

"Ay, if it's the Lord's will, Jamie, but am gey dune noo, an' Hendry's fell worn too."

Jamie, the boy that he was, said, "Dinna speak like that, mother," and Jess again put her hand on his head.

"Fine I ken, Jamie," she said, " 'at all my days on this earth, be they short or lang, I've you for a staff to lean on."

Ah, many years have gone since then, but if Jamie be living now he has still those words to swallow.

By and by Leeby went ben for the Bible, and put it into Hendry's hands. He slowly turned over the leaves to his favourite chapter, the fourteenth of John's Gospel. Always, on eventful occasions, did Hendry turn to the fourteenth of John.

"Let not your heart be troubled; ye believe in God, believe also in Me.

"In My Father's house are many mansions; if it were not so I would have told you. I go to prepare a place for you."

As Hendry raised his voice to read there was a great stillness in the kitchen. I do not know that I have been able to show in the most imperfect way what kind of man Hendry was. He was dense in many things, and the cleverness that was Jess's had been denied to him. He had less book-learning than most of those with whom he passed his days, and he had little skill in talk. I have not known a man more easily taken in by persons whose speech had two faces. But a more simple, modest, upright man, there never was in Thrums, and I shall always revere his memory.

"And if I go and prepare a place for you, I will come again, and receive you unto Myself; that where I am, there ye may be also."

The voice may have been monotonous. I have always thought that Hendry's reading of the Bible was the most solemn and impressive I have ever heard. He exulted in the fourteenth of John, pouring it forth like one whom it intoxicated while he read. He emphasized every other word; it was so real and grand to him.

We went upon our knees while Hendry prayed, all but Jess, who could not. Jamie buried his face in her lap. The words Hendry said were those he used every night. Some, perhaps, would have smiled at his prayer to God that we be not puffed up with riches nor with the things of this world. His head shook with emotion while he prayed, and he brought us very near to the throne of grace. "Do thou, O our God," he said, in conclusion, "spread Thy guiding hand over him whom in Thy great mercy Thou hast brought to us again, and do Thou guard him through the perils which come unto those that go down to the sea in ships. Let not our hearts be troubled, neither let them be afraid, for this is not our abiding home, and may we all meet in Thy house, where there are many mansions, and where there will be no last night. Amen."

It was a silent kitchen after that, though the lamp burned long in Jess's window. By its meagre light you may take a final glance at the little family; you will never see them together again.

CHAPTER XXI

THERE may be a few who care to know how the lives of Jess and Hendry ended. Leeby died in the back-end of the year I have been speaking of, and as I was snowed up in the school-house at the time, I heard the news from Gavin Birse too late to attend her funeral. She got her death on the commonty one day of sudden rain, when she had run out to bring in her washing, for the terrible cold she woke with next morning carried her off very quickly. Leeby did not blame Jamie for not coming to her, nor did I, for I knew that even in the presence of death the poor must drag their chains. He never got Hendry's letter with the news, and we know now that he was already in the hands of her who played the devil with his life. Before the spring came he had been lost to Jess.

"Them 'at has got sae mony blessin's mair than the generality," Hendry said to me one day, when Craigiebuckle had given me a lift into Thrums, "has nae shame if they would pray aye for mair.

163

The Lord has gi'en this hoose sae muckle, 'at to
pray for mair looks like no bein' thankfu' for what
we've got. Ay, but I canna help prayin' to Him
'at in His great mercy he'll take Jess afore me.
Noo 'at Leeby's gone, an' Jamie never lets us hear
frae him, I canna gulp doon the thocht o' Jess
bein' left alane."

This was a prayer that Hendry may be par-
doned for having so often in his heart, though God
did not think fit to grant it. In Thrums, when a
weaver died, his womenfolk had to take his seat
at the loom, and those who, by reason of infirmi-
ties, could not do so, went to a place the name of
which, I thank God, I am not compelled to write
in this chapter. I could not, even at this day,
have told any episodes in the life of Jess had it
ended in the poorhouse.

Hendry would probably have recovered from
the fever had not this terrible dread darkened his
intellect when he was still prostrate. He was
lying in the kitchen when I saw him last in life,
and his parting words must be sadder to the reader
than they were to me.

"Ay, richt ye are," he said, in a voice that had
become a child's; "I hae muckle, muckle, to be
thankfu' for, an' no the least is 'at baith me an' Jess
has aye belonged to a bural society. We hae nae
cause to be anxious aboot a' thing bein' dune re-
respectable aince we're gone. It was Jess 'at in-

sisted on oor joinin': a' the wisest things I ever did I was put up to by her."

I parted from Hendry, cheered by the doctor's report, but the old weaver died a few days afterwards. His end was mournful, yet I can recall it now as the not unworthy close of a good man's life. One night poor worn Jess had been helped ben into the room, Tibbie Birse having undertaken to sit up with Hendry. Jess slept for the first time for many days, and as the night was dying Tibbie fell asleep too. Hendry had been better than usual, lying quietly, Tibbie said, and the fever was gone. About three o'clock Tibbie woke and rose to mend the fire. Then she saw that Hendry was not in his bed.

Tibbie went ben the house in her stocking-soles, but Jess heard her.

" What is't, Tibbie ? " she asked, anxiously.

" Ou, it's no naething," Tibbie said, " he's lyin' rale quiet."

Then she went up to the attic. Hendry was not in the house.

She opened the door gently and stole out. It was not snowing, but there had been a heavy fall two days before, and the night was windy. A tearing gale had blown the upper part of the brae clear, and from T'nowhead's fields the snow was rising like smoke. Tibbie ran to the farm and woke up T'nowhead.

For an hour they looked in vain for Hendry. At last some one asked who was working in Elshioner's shop all night. This was the long earthen-floored room in which Hendry's loom stood with three others.

"It'll be Sanders Whamond likely," T'nowhead said, and the other men nodded.

But it happened that T'nowhead's Bell, who had flung on a wrapper, and hastened across to sit with Jess, heard of the light in Elshioner's shop.

"It's Hendry," she cried, and then every one moved toward the workshop.

The light at the diminutive, yarn-covered window was pale and dim, but Bell, who was at the house first, could make the most of a cruizey's glimmer.

"It's him," she said, and then, with swelling throat, she ran back to Jess.

The door of the workshop was wide open, held against the wall by the wind. T'nowhead and the others went in. The cruizey stood on the little window. Hendry's back was to the door, and he was leaning forward on the silent loom. He had been dead for some time, but his fellow-workers saw that he must have weaved for nearly an hour.

So it came about that for the last few months of her pilgrimage Jess was left alone. Yet I may not say that she was alone. Jamie, who should have been with her, was undergoing his own ordeal far away; where, we did not now even know. But though the poorhouse stands in Thrums, where all may see it, the neighbours did not think only of themselves.

Than Thomas Haggart there can scarcely have been a poorer man, but Tammas was the first to come forward with offer of help. To the day of Jess's death he did not once fail to carry her water to her in the morning, and the luxuriously living men of Thrums in those present days of pumps at every corner, can hardly realize what that meant. Often there were lines of people at the well by three o'clock in the morning, and each had to wait his turn. Tammas filled his own pitcher and pan, and then had to take his place at the end of the line with Jess's pitcher and pan, to wait his turn again. His own house was in the Tenements, far from the brae in winter time, but he always said to Jess it was " naething ava."

Every Saturday old Robbie Angus sent a bag of sticks and shavings from the saw-mill by his little son Rob, who was afterwards to become a man for speaking about at nights. Of all the friends that Jess and Hendry had, T'nowhead was the ablest to help, and the sweetest memory I have of the farmer and his wife is the delicate way they offered it. You who read will see Jess wince at the offer of charity. But the poor have fine feelings beneath the grime, as you will discover if you care to look for them, and when Jess said she would bake if any one would buy, you would wonder to hear how many kindly folk came to her door for scones.

She had the house to herself at nights, but Tibbie Birse was with her early in the morning, and other neighbours dropped in. Not for long did she have to wait the summons to the better home.

" Na," she said to the minister, who has told me that he was a better man from knowing her, " my thochts is no nane set on the vanities o' the world noo. I kenna hoo I could ever hae ha'en sic an ambeetion to hae thae stuff-bottomed chairs."

I have tried to keep away from Jamie, whom the neighbours sometimes upbraided in her presence. It is of him you who read would like to hear, and I cannot pretend that Jess did not sit at her window looking for him.

" Even when she was bakin'," Tibbie told me, " she aye had an eye on the brae. If Jamie had come at ony time when it was licht she would hae seen 'im as sune as he turned the corner."

" If he ever comes back, the sacket (rascal)," T'nowhead said to Jess, " we'll show 'im the door gey quick."

Jess just looked, and all the women knew how she would take Jamie to her arms.

We did not know of the London woman then, and Jess never knew of her. Jamie's mother

never for an hour allowed that he had become anything but the loving laddie of his youth.

"I ken 'im ower weel," she always said, "my
ain Jamie."

Toward the end she was sure he was dead. I
do not know when she first made up her mind
to this, nor whether it was not merely a phrase for
those who wanted to discuss him with her. I
know that she still sat at the window looking at
the elbow of the brae.

The minister was with her when she died. She
was in her chair, and he asked her, as was his custom, if there was any particular chapter which she
would like him to read. Since her husband's
death she had always asked for the fourteenth of
John, "Hendry's chapter," as it is still called among
a very few old people in Thrums. This time
she asked him to read the sixteenth chapter of
Genesis.

"When I came to the thirteenth verse," the
minister told me, "'And she called the name of
the Lord that spake unto her, Thou God seest me,'
she covered her face with her two hands, and said,
'Joey's text, Joey's text. Oh, but I grudged ye
sair, Joey.'"

"I shut the book," the minister said, "when I
came to the end of the chapter, and then I saw
that she was dead. It is my belief that her heart
broke one-and-twenty years ago."

CHAPTER XXII

JAMIE'S HOME-COMING

On a summer day, when the sun was in the weavers' workshops, and bairns hopped solemnly at the game of palaulays, or gaily shook their bottles of sugarelly water into a froth, Jamie came back. The first man to see him was Hookey Crewe, the post.

"When he came frae London," Hookey said afterwards at T'nowhead's pig-sty, "Jamie used to wait for me at Zoar, i' the north end o' Tilliedrum. He carried his box ower the market muir, an' sat on't at Zoar, waitin' for me to catch 'im up. Ay, the day afore yesterday me an' the powny was clatterin' by Zoar, when there was Jamie standin' in his identical place. He hadna nae box to sit upon, an' he was far frae bein' weel in order, but I kent 'im at aince, an' I saw 'at he was waitin' for me. So I drew up, an' waved my hand to 'im."

"I would hae drove straucht by 'im," said T'nowhead; "them 'at leaves their auld mother to want doesna deserve a lift."

"Ay, ye say that sittin' there," Hookey said;

170

"but, lads, I saw his face, an' as sure as death it was sic an' awfu' meeserable face 'at I couldna but pu' the powny up. Weel, he stood for the space o' a meenute lookin' straucht at me, as if he would like to come forrit but dauredna, an' syne he turned an' strided awa ower the muir like a huntit thing. I sat still i' the cart, an' when he was far awa he stoppit an' lookit again, but a' my cryin' wouldna bring him a step back, an' i' the end I drove on. I've thocht since syne 'at he didna ken whether his fowk was livin' or deid, an' was fleid to speir."

"He didna ken," said T'nowhead, "but the faut was his ain. It's ower late to be ta'en up aboot Jess noo."

"Ay, ay, T'nowhead," said Hookey, "it's aisy to you to speak like that. Ye didna see his face."

It is believed that Jamie walked from Tilliedrum, though no one is known to have met him on the road. Some two hours after the post left him he was seen by old Rob Angus at the sawmill.

"I was sawin' awa wi' a' my micht," Rob said, "an' little Rob was haudin' the booards, for they were silly but things, when something made me look at the window. It couldna hae been a tap on't, for the birds has used me to that, an' it would hardly be a shadow, for little Rob didna look up. Whatever it was, I stoppit i' the middle o' a

booard, an' lookit up, an' there I saw Jamie Mc-
Qumpha. He joukit back when our een met, but
I saw him weel; ay, it's a queer thing to say, but
he had the face o' a man 'at had come straucht
frae hell."

"I stood starin' at the window," Angus continued, "after he'd gone, an' Robbie cried oot to ken
what was the maiter wi' me. Ay, that brocht me
back to mysel, an' I hurried oot to look for Jamie,
but he wasna to be seen. That face gae me a
turn."

From the saw-mill to the house at the top of
the brae, some may remember, the road is up the
commonty. I do not think any one saw Jamie on
the commonty, though there were those to say they
met him.

"He gae me sic a look," a woman said, "'at
I was fleid an' ran hame," but she did not tell the
story until Jamie's home-coming had become a
legend.

There were many women hanging out their
washing on the commonty that day, and none of
them saw him. I think Jamie must have ap-
proached his old home by the fields, and probably
he held back until gloaming.

The young woman who was now mistress of the
house at the top of the brae both saw and spoke
with Jamie.

"Twa or three times," she said, "I had seen a

man walk quick up the brae an' by the door. It was gettin' dark, but I noticed 'at he was short an' thin, an' I would hae said he wasna nane weel if it hadna been at' he gaed by at sic a steek. He didna look our wy — at least no when he was close up, an' I set 'im doon for some ga'en aboot body. Na, I saw naething aboot 'im to be fleid at.

"The aucht o'clock bell was ringin' when I saw 'im to speak to. My twa-year-auld bairn was standin' aboot the door, an' I was makkin' some porridge for my man's supper when I heard the bairny skirlin'. She came runnin' in to the hoose an' hung i' my wrapper, an' she was hingin' there, when I gaed to the door to see what was wrang.

"It was the man I'd seen passin' the hoose. He was standin' at the gate, which, as a'body kens, is but sax steps frae the hoose, an' I wondered at 'im neither runnin' awa nor comin' forrit. I speired at 'im what he meant by terrifyin' a bairn, but he didna say naething. He juist stood. It was ower dark to see his face richt, an' I wasna nane ta'en aback yet, no till he spoke. Oh, but he had a fearsome word when he did speak. It was a kind o' like a man hoarse wi' a cauld, an' yet no that either.

"'Wha bides i' this hoose?' he said, ay standin there.

"'It's Davit Patullo's hoose,' I said, ' an' am the wife.'

" ' Whaur's Hendry McQumpha?' he speired.

" ' He's deid,' I said.

" He stood still for a fell while.

" ' An' his wife, Jess?' he said.

" ' She's deid, too,' I said.

" I thocht he gae a groan, but it may hae been the gate.

" ' There was a dochter, Leeby?' he said.

" ' Ay,' I said, ' she was ta'en first.'

" I saw 'im put up his hands to his face, an' he cried out, ' Leeby too!' an' syne he kind o' fell agin the dyke. I never kent 'im nor nane o' his fowk, but I had heard aboot them, an' I saw 'at it would be the son frae London. It wasna for me to judge 'im, an' I said to 'im would he no come in by an' tak a rest. I was nearer 'im by that time, an' it's an awfu' haver to say 'at he had a face to frichten fowk. It was a rale guid face, but no ava what a body would like to see on a young man. I felt mair like greetin' mysel when I saw his face than drawin' awa frae 'im.

" But he wouldna come in. ' Rest,' he said, like ane speakin' to 'imsel, ' na, there's nae mair rest for me.' I didna weel ken what mair to say to 'im, for he aye stood on, an' I wasna even sure 'at he saw me. He raised his heid when he heard me tellin' the bairn no to tear my wrapper.

" ' Dinna set yer heart ower muckle on that bairn,' he cried oot, sharp like. ' I was aince like her, an' I used to hing aboot my mother, too, in that very roady. Ay, I thocht I was fond o' her, an' she thocht it too. Tak' a care, wuman, 'at that bairn doesna grow up to murder ye.'

"He gae a lauch when he saw me tak haud o' the bairn, an' syne a' at aince he gaed awa quick. But he wasna far doon the brae when he turned an' came back.

"'Ye'll, mebbe, tell me," he said, richt low, 'if ye hae the furniture 'at used to be my mother's?'

"'Na,' I said, 'it was roupit, an' I kenna whaur the things gaed, for me an' my man comes frae Tilliedrum.'

"'Ye wouldna hae heard,' he said, 'wha got the muckle airm-chair 'at used to sit i' the kitchen i' the window 'at looks ower the brae?'

"'I couldna be sure,' I said, 'but there was an airm-chair at gaed to Tibbie Birse. If it was the ane ye mean, it a' gaed to bits, an' I think they burned it. It was gey dune.'

"'Ay,' he said, 'it was gey dune.'

"'There was the chairs ben i' the room,' he said, after a while.

"I said I thocht Sanders Elshioner had got them at a bargain because twa o' them was mended wi' glue, an' gey silly.

"'Ay, that's them,' he said, 'they were richt neat mended. It was my mother 'at glued them. I mind o' her makkin' the glue, an' warnin' me an' my father no to sit on them. There was the clock too, an' the stool 'at my mother got oot an' into her bed wi', an' the basket 'at Leeby carried when she gaed the errands. The straw was aff the handle, an' my father mended it wi' strings.'

"'I dinna ken,' I said, 'whaur nane o' thae gaed; but did yer mother hae a staff?'

"'A little staff,' he said; 'it was near black wi' age. She couldna gang frae the bed to her chair withoot it. It was broadened oot at the foot wi' her leanin' on't sae muckle.'

"'I've heard tell,' I said, ''at the dominie up i' Glen Quharity took awa the staff.'

"He didna speir for nae other thing. He had the gate in his hand, but I dinna think he kent 'at he was swingin't back an' forrit. At last he let it go.

"'That's a',' he said, 'I maun awa. Good-nicht, an' thank ye kindly.'

"I watched 'im till he gaed oot o' sicht. He gaed doon the brae."

We learnt afterwards from the gravedigger that some one spent great part of that night in the graveyard, and we believe it to have been Jamie. He walked up the glen to the school-house next forenoon, and I went out to meet him when I saw him coming down the path.

"Ay," he said, "it's me come back."

I wanted to take him into the house and speak

with him of his mother, but he would not cross the threshold.

" I came oot," he said, " to see if ye would gie me her staff — no 'at I deserve 't."

I brought out the staff and handed it to him, thinking that he and I would soon meet again. As he took it I saw that his eyes were sunk back into his head. Two great tears hung on his eye-lids, and his mouth closed in agony. He stared at me till the tears fell upon his cheeks, and then he went away.

That evening he was seen by many persons crossing the square. He went up the brae to his old home, and asked leave to go through the house for the last time. First he climbed up into the attic, and stood looking in, his feet still on the stair. Then he came down and stood at the door of the room, but he went into the kitchen.

" I'll ask one last favour o' ye, " he said to the woman: " I would like ye to leave me here alane for juist a little while."

" I gaed oot," the woman said, " meanin' to leave 'im to 'imsel', but my bairn wouldna come, an' he said, 'Never mind her,' so I left her wi' 'im, an' closed the door. He was in a lang time, but I never kent what he did, for the bairn juist aye greets when I speir at her.

" I watched 'im frae the corner window gang doon the brae till he came to the corner. I thocht he turned round there an' stood lookin' at the hoose. He would see me better than I saw him for my lamp was i' the window, whaur I've heard tell his mother keepit her cruizey. When my man came in I speired at 'im if he'd seen onybody standin' at the corner o' the brae, an' he said he thocht he'd seen somebody wi' a little staff in his hand. Davit gaed doon to see if he was aye there after supper-time, but he was gone."

Jamie was never again seen in Thrums.

AN EDINBURGH ELEVEN

I

LORD ROSEBERY

THE first time I ever saw Lord Rosebery was
in Edinburgh when I was a student, and I
flung a clod of earth at him. He was a peer;
those were my politics.

I missed him, and I have heard a good many
journalists say since then that he is a difficult man
to hit. One who began by liking him and is now
scornful, which is just the reverse process from
mine, told me the reason why. He had some
brochures to write on the Liberal leaders, and got
on nicely till he reached Lord Rosebery, where he
stuck. In vain he walked round his lordship,
looking for an opening. The man was naturally
indignant; he is the father of a family.

Lord Rosebery is forty-one years of age, and has
missed many opportunities of becoming the bosom
friend of Lord Randolph Churchill. They were
at Eton together and at Oxford, and have met
since. As a boy the Liberal played at horses, and
the Tory at running off with other boys' caps.
Lord Randolph was the more distinguished at the

University. One day a proctor ran him down in the streets smoking in his cap and gown. The undergraduate remarked on the changeability of the weather, but the proctor, gasping at such bravado, demanded his name and college. Lord Randolph failed to turn up next day at St. Edmund Hall to be lectured, but strolled to the Proctor's house about dinner-time. "Does a fellow, name of Moore, live here?" he asked. The footman contrived not to faint. "He do," he replied, severely; "but he are at dinner." "Ah! take him in my card," said the unabashed caller. The Merton books tell that for this the noble lord was fined ten pounds.

There was a time when Lord Rosebery would have reformed the House of Lords to a site nearer Newmarket. As politics took a firmer grip of him, it was Newmarket that seemed a long way off. One day at Edinburgh he realized the disadvantage of owning swift horses. His brougham had met him at Waverley Station to take him to Dalmeny. Lord Rosebery opened the door of the carriage to put in some papers, and then turned away. The coachman, too well bred to look round, heard the door shut, and thinking that his master was inside, set off at once. Pursuit was attempted, but what was there in Edinburgh streets to make up on those horses? The coachman drove seven miles, until he reached a point in the Dalmeny parks where it was his lordship's custom to alight and open a gate. Here the brougham stood for some minutes, awaiting Lord Rosebery's convenience. At last the coachman became uneasy and dismounted. His brain reeled when he saw an empty brougham. He could have sworn to seeing his lordship enter. There were his papers. What had happened? With a quaking hand the horses were turned, and, driving back, the coachman looked fearfully along the sides of the road. He met Lord Rosebery travelling in great good humour by the luggage omnibus.

Whatever is to be Lord Rosebery's future, he has reached that stage in a statesman's career when his opponents cease to question his capacity. His speeches showed him long ago a man of brilliant parts. His tenure of the Foreign Office proved him heavy metal. Were the Gladstonians to return to power, the other Cabinet posts might go anywhere, but the Foreign Secretary is arranged for. Where his predecessors had clouded their meaning in words till it was as wrapped up as a Mussulman's head, Lord Rosebery's were the straightforward dispatches of a man with his mind made up. German influence was spoken of; Count Herbert Bismarck had been seen shooting Lord Rosebery's partridges. This was the evidence: there has never been any other, except that German methods commended themselves to the

Minister rather than those of France. His relations with the French Government were cordial. "The talk of Bismarck's shadow behind Rosebery," a great French politician said lately, "I put aside with a smile; but how about the Jews?" Probably few persons realize what a power the Jews are in Europe, and in Lord Rosebery's position he is a strong man if he holds his own with them. Any fears on that ground have, I should say, been laid by his record at the Foreign Office.

Lord Rosebery had once a conversation with Prince Bismarck, to which, owing to some oversight, the Paris correspondent of the *Times* was not invited. M. Blowitz only smiled good-naturedly, and of course his report of the proceedings appeared all the same. Some time afterwards Lord Rosebery was introduced to this remarkable man, who, as is well known, carries Cabinet appointments in his pocket, and complimented him on his report. "Ah, it was all right, was it?" asked Blowitz, beaming. Lord Rosebery explained that any fault it had was that it was all wrong. "Then if Bismarck did not say that to you," said Blowitz, regally, "I know he intended to say it."

The "Uncrowned King of Scotland" is a title that has been made for Lord Rosebery, whose country has had faith in him from the beginning. Mr. Gladstone is the only other man who can make so many Scotsmen take politics as if it were the Highland Fling. Once when Lord Rosebery was firing an Edinburgh audience to the delirium point, an old man in the hall shouted out, "I dinna hear a word he says, but it's grand, it's grand!" During the first Midlothian campaign Mr. Gladstone and Lord Rosebery were the father and son of the Scottish people. Lord Rosebery rode into fame on the top of that wave, and he has kept his place in the hearts of the people, and in oleographs on their walls, ever since. In all Scottish matters he has the enthusiasm of a Burns dinner, and his humour enables him to pay compliments. When he says agreeable things to Scotsmen about their country, there is a twinkle in his eye and in theirs to which English scribes cannot give a meaning. He has unveiled so many Burns statues that an American lecturess explains, "Curious thing, but I feel somehow I am connected with Lord Rosebery. I go to a place and deliver a lecture on Burns; they collect subscriptions for a statue, and he unveils it." Such is the delight of the Scottish students in Lord Rosebery, that he may be said to have made the triumphal tour of the northern universities as their Lord Rector; he lost the post in Glasgow lately through a quibble, but had the honour with the votes. His address to the Edinburgh undergraduates on "Patriotism" was the best thing he ever did outside politics, and made the students his for life. Some of them had smuggled into the hall a chair with "Gaelic chair" placarded on it, and the Lord Rector unwittingly played into their hands. In a noble peroration he exhorted his hearers to high aims in life. "Raise your country," he exclaimed (cheers); "raise yourselves" (renewed cheering); "raise your university" (thunders of applause). From the back of the hall came a solemn voice, "Raise the chair!" Up went the Gaelic chair.

Even Lord Rosebery's views on Imperial Federation can become a compliment to Scotland. Having been all over the world himself, and felt how he grew on his travels, Lord Rosebery maintains that every British statesman should visit India and the Colonies. He said that first at a semi-public dinner in the country — and here I may mention that on such occasions he has begun his speeches less frequently than any other prominent politician with a statement that others could be got to discharge the duty better; in other words, he has several times omitted this introduction. On his return to London he was told that his colleagues in the Administration had been seeing how his scheme would work out. "We found that if your rule were enforced, the Cabinet would consist of yourself and Childers." "This would be an ideal Cabinet," Lord Rosebery subsequently remarked in Edinburgh, "for it would be entirely

Scottish ; " Mr. Childers being member for a Scottish constituency.

The present unhappy division of the Liberal
party has made enemies of friends for no leading
man so little as for Lord Rosebery. There are
forces working against him, no doubt, in compar-
atively high places, but the Unionists have kept
their respect for him. His views may be wrong,
but he is about the only Liberal leader, with the
noble exception of Lord Hartington, of whom
troublous times have not rasped the temper.
Though a great reader, he is not a literary man like
Mr. Morley, who would, however, be making
phrases where Lord Rosebery would make laws.
Sir William Harcourt has been spoken of as a
possible Prime Minister, but surely it will never
come to that. If Mr. Gladstone's successor is
chosen from those who have followed him on the
Home Rule question, he probably was not rash in
himself naming Lord Rosebery.

Lord Rosebery could not now step up without
stepping into the Premiership. His humour,
which is his most obvious faculty, has been a prop
to him many a time ere now, but, if I was his ad-
viser, I should tell him that it had served its pur-
pose. There are a great many excellent people
who shake their heads over it in a man who has
become a power in the land. " Let us be grave,"
said Dr. Johnson once to a merry companion, " for

here comes a fool." In an unknown novel there is a character who says of himself that " he is not stupid enough ever to be a great man." I happen to know that this reflection was evolved by the author out of thinking over Lord Rosebery. It is not easy for a bright man to be heavy, and Lord Rosebery's humour is so spontaneous that if a joke is made in their company he has always finished laughing before Lord Hartington begins. Perhaps when Lord Rosebery is on the point of letting his humour run off with him in a public speech he could recover his solemnity by thinking of the *Examiner*.

II

PROFESSOR MASSON

THOUGH a man might, to my mind, be better employed than in going to college, it is his own fault if he does not strike on some one there who sends his life off at a new angle. If, as I take it, the glory of a professor is to give elastic minds their proper bent, Masson is a name his country will retain a grip of. There are men who are good to think of, and as a rule we only know them from their books. Something of our pride in life would go with their fall. To have one such professor at a time is the most a university can hope of human nature, so Edinburgh need not expect another just yet. These, of course, are only to be taken as the reminiscences of a student. I seem to remember everything Masson said, and the way he said it.

Having immediately before taken lodgings in a crow's nest, my first sight of Masson was specially impressive. It was the opening of the session, when fees were paid, and a whisper ran round the quadrangle that Masson had set off home with three hundred one-pound notes stuffed into his trouser pockets. There was a solemn swell of awestruck students to the gates, and some of us could not help following him. He took his pockets coolly. When he stopped it was at a second-hand book-stall, where he rummaged for a long time. Eventually he pounced upon a dusty, draggled little volume, and went off proudly with it beneath his arm. He seemed to look suspiciously at strangers now, but it was not the money but the book he was keeping guard over. His pockets, however, were unmistakably bulging out. I resolved to go in for literature.

Masson, however, always comes to my memory first knocking nails into his desk or trying to tear the gas-bracket from its socket. He said that the Danes scattered over England, taking such a hold as a nail takes when it is driven into wood. For the moment he saw his desk turned into England; he whirled an invisible hammer in the air, and down it came on the desk with a crash. No one who has sat under Masson can forget how the Danes nailed themselves upon England. His desk is thick with their tombstones. It was when his mind groped for an image that he clutched the bracket. He seemed to tear his good things out of it. Silence overcame the class. Some were fascinated by the man; others trembled for the bracket. It shook, groaned, and yielded. Masson said another of the things that made his lectures literature; the crisis was passed; and everybody breathed again.

He masters a subject by letting it master him; for though his critical reputation is built on honesty, it is his enthusiasm that makes his work warm with life. Sometimes he entered the class-room so full of what he had to say that he began before he reached his desk. If he was in the middle of a peroration when the bell rang, even the back-benches forgot to empty. There were the inevitable students to whom literature is a trial, and sometimes they call attention to their sufferings by a scraping of the feet. Then the professor tried to fix his eyeglass on them, and when it worked properly they were transfixed. As a rule, however, it required so many adjustments that by the time his eye took hold of it he had remembered that students were made so, and his indignation went. Then, with the light in his eye that some photographer ought to catch, he would hope that his lecture was not disturbing their conversation. It was characteristic of his passion for being just that when he had criticised some writer severely he would remember that the back-benches could not understand that criticism and admiration might go together, unless they were told so again.

The test of a sensitive man is that he is careful of wounding the feelings of others. Once, I remember, a student was reading a passage aloud, assuming at the same time such an attitude that the Professor could not help remarking that he looked like a teapot. It was exactly what he did look like, and the class applauded. But next moment Masson had apologized for being personal. Such reminiscences are what make the old literature classroom to thousands of graduates a delight to think of.

When the news of Carlyle's death reached the room, Masson could not go on with his lecture. Every one knows what Carlyle has said of him; and no one who has heard it will ever forget what he has said of Carlyle. Here were two men who understood each other. One of the Carlylean pictures one loves to dwell on shows them smoking together, with nothing breaking the pauses but Mrs. Carlyle's needles. Carlyle told Masson how he gave up smoking and then took to it again. He had walked from Dumfriesshire to Edinburgh to consult a doctor about his health, and was advised to lose his pipe. He smoked no more, but his health did not improve, and then one day he walked in a wood. At the foot of a tree lay a pipe, a tobacco pouch, a match-box. He saw clearly that this was a case of Providential interference, and from that moment he smoked again. There the Professor's story stops. I have no doubt, though, that he nodded his head when Carlyle explained what the pipe and tobacco were doing there.

Masson's " Milton " is, of course, his great work, but for sympathetic analysis I know nothing to surpass his " Chatterton." Lecturing on Chatterton one day, he remarked, with a slight hesitation, that had the poet mixed a little more in company and — and smoked, his morbidness would not have poisoned him. That turned my thoughts to smoking, because I meant to be a Chatterton, but greater. Since then the professor has warned me against smoking too much. He was smoking at the time.

This is no place to follow Masson's career, nor to discuss his work. To reach his position one ought to know his definition of a man-of-letters. It is curious, and, like most of his departures from the generally accepted, sticks to the memory. By a man-of-letters he does not mean the poet, for instance, who is all soul, so much as the strong-brained writer whose guardian angel is a fine sanity. He used to mention John Skelton, the Wolsey satirist, and Sir David Lindsay, as typical men-of-letters from this point of view, and it is as a man-of-letters of that class that Masson is best considered. In an age of many whipper-snappers in criticism he is something of a Gulliver.

The students in that class liked to see their professor as well as hear him. I let my hair grow long because it only annoyed other people, and one day there was dropped into my hand a note containing sixpence and the words: "The students sitting behind you present their compliments, and beg that you will get your hair cut with the enclosed, as it interferes with their view of the professor."

Masson, when he edited "Macmillan's," had all the best men round him. His talk of Thackeray is specially interesting, but he always holds that in conversation Douglas Jerrold was unapproachable. Jerrold told him a good story of his sea-faring days. His ship was lying off Gibraltar, and for some hours Jerrold, though only a midshipman, was left in charge. Some of the sailors begged to get ashore, and he let them, on the promise that they would bring him back some oranges. One of them disappeared, and the midshipman suffered for it. More than twenty years afterwards Jerrold was looking in at a window in the Strand when he seemed to know the face of a weather-beaten man who was doing the same thing. Suddenly he remembered, and put his hand on the other's shoulder. "My man," he said, "you have been a long time with those oranges!" The sailor recognized him, turned white, and took to his heels. There is, too, the story of how Dickens and Jerrold made up their quarrel at the Garrick Club. It was the occasion on which Masson first met the author of "Pickwick." Dickens and Jerrold had not spoken for a year, and they both hap-

pened to have friends at dinner in the strangers'
room, Masson being Jerrold's guest. The two
hosts sat back to back, but did not address each
other, though the conversation was general. At
last Jerrold could stand it no longer. Turning, he
exclaimed, " Charley, my boy, how are you?"
Dickens wheeled round and grasped his hand.

Many persons must have noticed that, in appearance, Masson is becoming more and more like
Carlyle every year. How would you account for
it? It is a thing his old students often discuss
when they meet, especially those of them who,
when at college, made up their minds to dedicate
their first book to him. The reason they seldom
do it is because the book does not seem good
enough.

III

PROFESSOR JOHN STUART BLACKIE

LATELY I was told that Blackie — one does not say Mr. Cromwell — is no longer Professor of Greek in Edinburgh University. What nonsense some people talk. As if Blackie were not part of the building. In his class one day he spoke touchingly of the time when he would have to join Socrates in the Elysian fields. A student cheered — no one knows why. "It won't be for some time yet," added John Stuart.

Blackie takes his ease at home in a dressing-gown and straw hat. This shows that his plaid really does come off. "My occupation nowadays," he said to me recently, "is business, blethers, bothers, beggars, and backgammon." He has also started a profession of going to public meetings, and hurrying home to write letters to the newspapers about them. When the editor shakes the manuscript a sonnet falls out. I think I remember the Professor saying that he had never made five shillings by his verses. To my mind they are worth more than that.

PROFESSOR JOHN STUART BLACKIE

Though he has explained them frequently, there is still confusion about Blackie's politics. At Manchester they thought he was a Tory, and invited him to address them on that understanding. "I fancy I astonished them," the Professor said to me. This is quite possible. Then he was mistaken for a Liberal.

The fact is that Blackie is a philosopher who follows the golden mean. He sees this himself. A philosopher who follows the golden mean is thus a man who runs zig-zag between two extremes. You will observe that he who does this is some time before he arrives anywhere.

The Professor has said that he has the strongest lungs in Scotland. Of the many compliments that might well be paid him, not the least worthy would be this, that he is as healthy mentally as physically. Mrs. Norton begins a novel with the remark that one of the finest sights conceivable is a well-preserved gentleman of middle-age. It will be some time yet before Blackie reaches middle-age, but there must be something wrong with you if you can look at him without feeling refreshed. Did you ever watch him marching along Princes Street on a warm day, when every other person was broiling in the sun? His head is well thrown back, the staff, grasped in the middle, jerks back and forward like a weaver's shuttle, and the plaid flies in the breeze. Other people's clothes are hanging limp. Blackie carries his breeze with him.

A year or two ago Mr. Gladstone, when at Dalmeny, pointed out that he had the advantage over Blackie in being of both Highland and Lowland extraction. The Professor, however, is as Scotch as the thistle or his native hills, and Mr. Gladstone, quite justifiably, considers him the most outstanding of living Scotsmen. Blackie is not quite sure himself. Not long ago I heard him read a preface to a life of Mr. Gladstone that was being printed at Smyrna in modern Greek. He told his readers to remember that Mr. Gladstone was a great scholar and an upright statesman. They would find it easy to do this if they first remembered that he was Scottish.

The *World* included Blackie in its list of "Celebrities at Home." It said that the door was opened by a red-headed lassie. That was probably meant for local colour, and it amused every one who knew Mrs. Blackie. The Professor is one of the most genial of men, and will show you to your room himself, talking six languages. This tends to make the conversation one-sided, but he does not mind that. He still writes a good deal, spending several hours in his library daily, and his talk is as brilliant as ever. His writing nowadays is less sustained than it was, and he prefers flitting from one subject to another to evolving a great work. When he dips his pen into an ink-pot it at once writes a sonnet — so strong is the force of habit. Recently he wrote a page about Carlyle in a little book issued by the Edinburgh students' bazaar committee. In this he reproved Carlyle for having "bias." Blackie wonders why people should have bias.

Some readers of this may in their student days have been invited to the Greek professor's house to breakfast without knowing why they were selected from among so many. It was not, as they are probably aware, because of their classical attainments, for they were too thoughtful to be in the prize-list; nor was it because of the charm of their manners or the fascination of their conversation. When the Professor noticed any physical peculiarity about a student, such as a lisp, or a glass eye, or one leg longer than the other, or a broken nose, he was at once struck by it, and asked him to breakfast. They were very lively breakfasts, the eggs being served in tureens; but sometimes it was a collection of the maimed and crooked, and one person at the table — not the host himself — used to tremble lest, making mirrors of each other, the guests should see why they were invited.

Sometimes, instead of asking a student to break-fast, Blackie would instruct another student to request his company to tea. Then the two students were told to talk about paulo-post futures in the cool of the evening, and to read their Greek Testament and to go to the pantomime. The Professor never tired of giving his students advice about the preservation of their bodily health. He strongly recommended a cold bath at six o'clock every morning. In winter, he remarked genially, you can break the ice with a hammer. According to himself, only one enthusiast seems to have followed his advice, and he died.

In Blackie's classroom there used to be a demonstration every time he mentioned the name of a distinguished politician. Whether the demonstration took the Professor by surprise, or whether he waited for it, will never, perhaps, be known. But Blackie at least put out the gleam in his eye, and looked as if he were angry. "I will say Beaconsfield," he would exclaim (cheers and hisses). "Beaconsfield" (uproar). Then he would stride forward, and, seizing the railing, announce his intention of saying Beaconsfield until every goose in the room was tired of cackling. ("Question.") "Beaconsfield." ("No, no.") "Beaconsfield." ("Hear, hear," and shouts of "Gladstone.") "Beaconsfield." ("Three cheers for Dizzy.") Eventually the class would be dismissed as — (1) idiots, (2) a bear garden, (3) a flock of sheep, (4) a pack of numskulls, (5) hissing serpents. The professor would retire, apparently fuming, to his anteroom, and five minutes afterwards he would be playing himself down the North Bridge on imaginary bagpipes. This sort of thing added a sauce to all academic sessions. There was a notebook also, which appeared year after year. It contained the Professor's jokes of a former session, carefully classified by an admiring student. It was handed down from one year's men to the next, and thus if Blackie began to make a joke about haggis, the possessor of the book had only swiftly to turn to the H's, find what the joke was, and send it along the class quicker than the professor could speak it.

In the old days the Greek professor recited a poem in honour of the end of the session. He composed it himself, and, as known to me, it took the form of a graduate's farewell to his Alma Mater. Sometimes he would knock a map down as if overcome with emotion, and at critical moments a student in the back benches would accompany him on a penny trumpet. Now, I believe, the Hellenic Club takes the place of the classroom. All the eminent persons in Edinburgh attend its meetings, and Blackie, the Athenian, is in the chair. The policeman in Douglas Crescent looks skeered when you ask him what takes place on these occasions. It is generally understood that toward the end of the meeting they agree to read Greek next time.

IV

HERE is a true story that the general reader may jump, as it is intended for Professor Calderwood himself. Some years ago an English daily paper reviewed a book entitled "A Handbook of Moral Philosophy." The Professor knows the work. The "notice" was done by the junior reporter, to whom philosophical treatises are generally entrusted. He dealt leniently, on the whole, with Professor Calderwood, even giving him a word of encouragement here and there. Still the criticism was severe. The reviewer subsequently went to Edinburgh University, and came out 144th in the class of Moral Philosophy.

That student is now, I believe, on friendly terms with Professor Calderwood, but has never told him this story. I fancy the Professor would like to know his name. It may, perhaps, be reached in this way. He was the young gentleman who went to his classes the first day in a black coat and silk hat, and was cheered round the quadrangle by a body of admiring fellow-students, who took him for a professor.

PROFESSOR CALDERWOOD

Calderwood contrives to get himself more in touch with the mass of his students than some of his fellow-professors, partly because he puts a high ideal before himself, and to some extent because his subject is one that Scottish students revel in. Long before they join his class they know that they are moral philosophers; indeed, they are sometimes surer of it before they enrol than afterwards. Their essays begin in some such fashion as this — "In joining issue with Reid, I wish to take no unfair advantage of my antagonist"; or "Kant is sadly at fault when he says that"; or "It is strange that a man of Locke's attainments should have been blind to the fact." When the Professor reads out these tit-bits to the class his eyes twinkle. Some students, of course, are not such keen philosophers as others. Does Professor Calderwood remember the one who was never struck by anything in moral philosophy until he learned by accident that Descartes lay in bed till about twelve o'clock every morning? Then it dawned on him that he, too, must have been a philosopher all his life without knowing it. One year a father and son were in the class. The father got so excited over volition and the line that divides right from wrong, that he wrenched the desk before him from its sockets and hit it triumphantly, meaning that he and the Professor were at one. He was generally admired by his fellow-students, because he was the only one in the class who could cry out " Hear, hear," and even "question," without blushing. The son, on the other hand, was *blasé*, and would have been an agnostic, only he could never remember the name. Once a week Calderwood turns his class into a debating society, and argues things out with his students. This field-day is a joy to them. Some of them spend the six days previous in preparing posers. The worst of the Professor is that he never sees that they are posers. What is the use of getting up a question of the most subtle kind, when he answers it right away? It makes you sit down quite suddenly. There is an occasional student who tries to convert liberty of speech on the discussion day into license, and of him the Professor makes short work. The student means to turn the laugh on Calderwood, and then Calderwood takes advantage of him, and the other students laugh at the wrong person. It is the older students, as a rule, who are most violently agitated over these philosophical debates. One with a beard cracks his fingers, after the manner of a child in a village school that knows who won the battle of Bannockburn, and feels that he must burst if he does not let it out at once. A bald-headed man rises every minute to put a question, and then sits down, looking stupid. He has been trying so hard to remember what it is, that he has forgotten. There is a legend of two who quarrelled over the Will and fought it out on Arthur's Seat.

One year, however, a boy of sixteen or so, with a squeaky voice and a stammer, was Calderwood's severest critic. He sat on the back bench, and what he wanted to know was something about the infinite. Every discussion day he took advantage of a lull in the debate to squeak out, "With regard to the infinite," and then could never get any further. No one ever discovered what he wanted enlightenment on about the infinite. He grew despondent as the session wore on, but courageously stuck to his point. Probably he is a soured man now. For purposes of exposition Calderwood has a black board in his lecture-room, on which he chalks circles that represent the feelings and the will, with arrows shooting between them. In my class there was a boy, a very little boy, who had been a dux at school and was a dunce at college. He could not make moral philosophy out at all, but did his best. Here were his complete notes for one day : —" Edinburgh University, class of Moral Philosophy, Professor Calderwood, Lecture 64, Jan. 11, 18—. You rub out the arrow, and there is only the circle left."

Professor Calderwood is passionately fond of music, as those who visit at his house know. He is of opinion that there is a great deal of moral philosophy in " The Dead March in Saul." Once he said something to that effect in his class, adding enthusiastically that he could excuse the absence of a student who had been away hearing "The Dead March in Saul." After that he received a good many letters from students, worded in this way: "Mr. McNaughton (bench 7) presents his compliments to Professor Calderwood, and begs to state that his absence from the class yesterday was owing to his being elsewhere, hearing 'The Dead March in Saul.'" "Dear Professor Calderwood — I regret my absence from the lecture to-day, but hope you will overlook it, as I was unavoidably detained at home, practising 'The Dead March in Saul.'— Yours truly, PETER WEBSTER." "Professor Calderwood,— Dear Sir,— As I was coming to the lecture to-day, I heard 'The Dead March in Saul' being played in the street. You will, I am sure, make allowance for my non-attendance at the class, as I was too much affected to come. It is indeed a grand march.— Yours faithfully, JOHN ROBBIE." "The students whose names are subjoined thank the Professor of Moral Philosophy most cordially for his remarks on the elevating power of music. They have been encouraged thereby to start a class for the proper study of the impressive and solemn march to which he called special attention, and hope he will excuse them, should their practisings occasionally prevent their attendance at the Friday lectures."

PROFESSOR CALDERWOOD

Professor Calderwood does not lecture on " The Dead March in Saul " now.

The class of Moral Philosophy is not for the few, but the many. Some professors do not mind what becomes of the nine students, so long as they can force on every tenth. Calderwood, however, considers it his duty to carry the whole class along with him, and it is, as a consequence, almost impossible to fall behind. The lectures are not delivered, in the ordinary sense, but dictated. Having explained the subject of the day with the lucidity that is this professor's peculiar gift, he condenses his remarks into a proposition. It is as if a minister ended his sermon with the text. Thus :—" Proposition 34. Man is born into the world—(You have got that? See that you have all got it.) Man is born into the world with a capacity—with a capacity—" (Anxious student : " If you please, Professor, where did you say man was born into ? ") " Into the world, with a capacity to distinguish " —(" With a what, sir ? ") —" with a capacity to distinguish "— (Student : " Who is born into the world ? ") " Perhaps I have been reading too quickly. Man is born into the world with a capacity to distinguish between— distinguish between (student shuts his book, thinking that completes the proposition) — distinguish between right and wrong — right — and wrong. You have all got Proposition 34, gentlemen ? "

Once Calderwood was questioning a student about a proposition to see that he thoroughly understood it. "Give an illustration," suggested the Professor. The student took the case of a murderer. "Very good," said the Professor. "Now give me another illustration." The student pondered for a little. "Well," he said at length, "take the case of another murderer."

Professor Calderwood has such an exceptional interest in his students that he asks every one of them to his house. This is but one of many things that make him generally popular; he also invites his ladies' class to meet them. The lady whom you take down to supper suggests Proposition 41 as a nice thing to talk about, and asks what you think of the metaphysics of ethics. Professor Calderwood sees the ladies into the cabs himself. It is the only thing I ever heard against him.

V

Just as I opened my desk to write enthusiastically of Tait, I remembered having recently deciphered a pencil note about him, in my own handwriting, on the cover of Masson's "Chronological List," which I still keep by me. I turned to the note to see if there was life in it yet. "Walls," it says, "got 2s. for T. and T. at Brown's, 16, Walker-street." I don't recall Walls, but T. and T. was short for "Thomson and Tait's Elements of Natural Philosophy" (Elements!), better known in my year as the "Student's First Glimpse of Hades." Evidently Walls sold his copy, but why did I take such note of the address? I fear T. and T. is one of the Books Which Have Helped Me. This somewhat damps my ardour.

When Tait was at Cambridge it was flung in the face of the mathematicians that they never stood high in Scriptural knowledge. Tait and another were the two of whom one must be first wrangler, and they agreed privately to wipe this stigma from mathematics. They did it by taking

year about the prize which was said to hang out
of their reach. It is always interesting to know of
professors who have done well in Biblical knowledge. All Scottish students at the English Universities are not so successful. I knew a Snell
man who was sent back from the Oxford entrance
exam., and he always held himself that the Biblical
questions had done it.

Turner is said by medicals to be the finest lecturer in the University. He will never be that so
long as Tait is in the Natural Philosophy chair.
Never, I think, can there have been a more superb
demonstrator. I have his burly figure before me.
The small twinkling eyes had a fascinating gleam
in them; he could concentrate them until they
held the object looked at; when they flashed round
the room he seemed to have drawn a rapier. I
have seen a man fall back in alarm under Tait's
eyes, though there were a dozen benches between
them. These eyes could be merry as a boy's,
though, as when he turned a tube of water on
students who would insist on crowding too near an
experiment, for Tait's was the humor of high
spirits. I could conceive him at marbles still, and
feeling annoyed at defeat. He could not fancy
anything much funnier than a man missing his
chair. Outside his own subject he is not, one feels,
a six-footer. When Mr. R. L. Stevenson's me-
moir of the late Mr. Fleeming Jenkin was pub-

lished, Tait said at great length that he did not like it; he would have had the sketch by a scientific man.   But though scientists may be the only men nowadays who have anything to say, they are also the only men who can't say it.   Scientific men out of their sphere know for a fact that novels are not true, so they draw back from novelists who write biography.   Professor Tait and Mr. Stevenson are both men of note, who walk different ways, and when they meet neither likes to take the curbstone.   If they were tied together for life in a three-legged race, which would suffer the more?

But if Tait's science weighs him to the earth, he has a genius for sticking to his subject, and I am lost in admiration every time I bring back his lectures.   It comes as natural to his old students to say when they meet, "What a lecturer Tait was!" as to Englishmen to joke about the bagpipes.   It is not possible to draw a perfect circle, Chrystal used to say, after drawing a very fine one.   To the same extent it was not possible for Tait never to fail in his experiments.   The atmosphere would be too much for him once in a session, or there were other hostile influences at work.   Tait warned us of these before proceeding to experiment, but we merely smiled.   We believed in him as though he were a Bradshaw announcing that he would not be held responsible for possible errors.

I had forgotten Lindsay; "the mother may forget her child." As I write he has slipped back into his chair on the Professor's right, and I could photograph him now in his brown suit. Lindsay was the imperturbable man who assisted Tait in his experiments, and his father held the post before him. When there were many of us together, we could applaud Lindsay with burlesque exaggeration, and he treated us good-humouredly, as making something considerable between us. But I once had to face Lindsay alone, in quest of my certificate; and suddenly he towered above me, as a waiter may grow tall when you find that you have not money enough to pay the bill. He treated me most kindly; did not reply, of course, but got the certificate, and handed it to me as a cashier contemptuously shovels you your pile of gold. Long ago I pasted up a crack in my window with the certificate, but it said, I remember, that I had behaved respectably— so far as I had come under the eyes of the Professor. Tait was always an enthusiast.

We have been keeping Lindsay waiting. When he had nothing special to do he sat indifferently in his chair, with the face of a precentor after the sermon has begun. But though it was not very likely that Lindsay would pay much attention to talk about such playthings as the laws of Nature, his fingers went out in the direction of the Professor when the experiments began. Then he was not the precentor; he was a minister in one of the pews. Lindsay was an inscrutable man, and I shall not dare to say that he even half-wished to see Tait fail. He only looked on, ready for any emergency; but if the experiment would not come off, he was as quick to go to the Professor's assistance as a member of Parliament is to begin when he has caught the Speaker's eye. Perhaps Tait would have none of his aid, or pushed the mechanism for the experiment from him — an intimation to Lindsay to carry it quickly to the ante-room. Do you think Lindsay read the instructions so? Let me tell you that your mind fails to seize hold of Lindsay. He marched the machine out of Tait's vicinity as a mother may push her erring boy away from his father's arms, to take him to her heart as soon as the door is closed. Lindsay took the machine to his seat, and laid it before him on the desk with well-concealed apathy. Tait would flash his eye to the right to see what Lindsay was after, and there was Lindsay sitting with his arms folded. The Professor's lecture resumed its way, and then out went Lindsay's hands to the machine. Here he tried a wheel; again he turned a screw; in time he had the machine ready for another trial. No one was looking his way, when suddenly there was a whizz — bang, bang. All eyes were turned upon Lindsay, the Professor's among them. A cheer broke out as we realized that Lindsay had done the experiment. Was he flushed with triumph? Not a bit of it; he was again sitting with his arms folded. A Glasgow merchant of modest manners, when cross-examined in a law court, stated that he had a considerable monetary interest in a certain concern. "How much do you mean by a 'considerable monetary interest'?" demanded the contemptuous barrister who was cross-examining him. "Oh," said the witness, humbly, "a maiter o' a million an' a half—or, say, twa million." That Glasgow man in the witness-box is the only person I can think of when looking about me for a parallel to Lindsay. While the Professor eyed him and the students deliriously beat the floor, Lindsay quietly gathered the mechanism together and carried it to the ante-room. His head was not flung back nor his chest forward, like one who walked to music. In his hour of triumph he was still imperturbable. I lie back in my chair to-day, after the lapse of years, and ask myself again, How did Lindsay behave after he entered the ante-room, shutting the door behind him? Did he give way? There is no one to say. When he returned to the classroom he wore his familiar face; a man to ponder over.

There is a legend about the Natural Philosophy classroom—the period long antecedent to Tait. The Professor, annoyed by a habit students had got into of leaving their hats on his desk, announced that the next hat placed there would be cut in pieces by him in presence of the class. The warning had its effect, until one day when the Professor was called for a few minutes from the room. An undergraduate, to whom the natural sciences, unrelieved, were a monotonous study, slipped into the ante-room, from which he emerged with the Professor's hat. This he placed on the desk, and then stole in a panic to his seat. An awe fell upon the class. The Professor returned, but when he saw the hat he stopped. He showed no anger. "Gentlemen," he said, "I told you what would happen if you again disobeyed my orders." Quite blandly he took a pen-knife from his pocket, slit the hat into several pieces, and flung them into the sink. While the hat was under the knife the students forgot to demonstrate, but as it splashed into the sink they gave forth a true British cheer. The end.

Close to the door of the Natural Philosophy room is a window that in my memory will ever be sacred to a janitor. The janitors of the University were of varied interest, from the merry one who treated us as if we were his equals, and the soldier who sometimes looked as if he would like to mow us down, to the Head Man of All, whose name I dare not write, though I can whisper it. The janitor at the window, however, sat there through the long evenings while the Debating Society (of which

I was a member) looked after affairs of State in an adjoining room. We were the smallest society in the University and the longest-winded, and I was once nearly expelled for not paying my subscription. Our grand debate was, " Is the policy of the Government worthy the confidence of this Society?" and we also read about six essays yearly on " The Genius of Robert Burns "; but it was on private business that we came out strongest. The question that agitated us most was whether the meetings should be opened with prayer, and the men who thought they should would not so much as look at the men who thought they should not. When the janitor was told that we had begun our private business he returned to his window and slept. His great day was when we could not form a quorum, which happened now and then.

Gregory was a member of that society: what has become of Gregory? He was one of those men who professors say have a brilliant future before them, and who have not since been heard of. Morton, another member, was of a different stamp. He led in the debate on " Beauty of the Mind v. Beauty of the Body." His writhing contempt for the beauty that is only skin deep is not to be forgotten. How noble were his rhapsodies on the beauty of the mind! And when he went to Calderwood's to supper, how quick he was to pick out the prettiest girl, who took ten per cent. in Moral

Philosophy, and to sit beside her all the evening. Morton had a way of calling on his friends the night before a degree examination to ask them to put him up to as much as would pull him through.

Tait used to get greatly excited over the rectorial elections, and if he could have disguised himself, would have liked, I think, to join in the fight round the Brewster statue. He would have bled for the Conservative cause, as his utterances on University reform have shown. The reformers have some cause for thinking that Tait is a greater man in his classroom than when he addresses the graduates. He has said that the less his students know of his subject when they join his class, the less, probably, they will have to unlearn. Such views are behind the times that feed their children on geographical biscuits in educational nurseries with astronomical ceilings and historical wall-papers.

VI

PROFESSOR CAMPBELL FRASER

NOT long ago I was back in the Old University — how well I remember pointing it out as the gaol to a stranger who had asked me to show him round. I was in one of the library ante-rooms, when some one knocked, and I looked up, to see Campbell Fraser framed in the doorway. I had not looked on that venerable figure for half a dozen years. I had forgotten all my metaphysics. Yet it all came back with a rush. I was on my feet, wondering if I existed strictly so-called.

Calderwood and Fraser had both their followings. The moral philosophers wore an air of certainty, for they knew that if they stuck to Calderwood he would pull them through. You cannot lose yourself in the back-garden. But the metaphysicians had their doubts. Fraser led them into strange places, and said he would meet them there again next day. They wandered to their lodgings, and got into difficulties with their landlady for saying that she was only an aggregate of sense phenomena. Fraser was rather a hazardous cure for weak intellects. Young men whose anchor had been certainty of themselves went into that class floating buoyantly on the sea of facts, and came out all adrift — on the sea of theory — in an open boat — rudderless — one oar — the boat scuttled. How could they think there was any chance for them, when the Professor was not even sure of himself? I see him rising in a daze from his chair and putting his hands through his hair. " Do I exist," he said, thoughtfully, " strictly so-called? " The students (if it was the beginning of the session) looked a littled startled. This was a matter that had not previously disturbed them. Still, if the Professor was in doubt, there must be something in it. He began to argue it out, and an uncomfortable silence held the room in awe. If he did not exist, the chances were that they did not exist either. It was thus a personal question. The Professor glanced round slowly for an illustration. " Am I a table? " A pained look travelled over the class. Was it just possible that they were all tables? It is no wonder that the students who do not go to the bottom during their first month of metaphysics begin to give themselves airs strictly so-called. In the privacy of their room at the top of the house they pinch themselves to see if they are still there.

He would, I think, be a sorry creature who did not find something to admire in Campbell Fraser.

Metaphysics may not trouble you, as it troubles him, but you do not sit under the man without seeing his transparent honesty and feeling that he is genuine. In appearance and in habit of thought he is an ideal philosopher, and his communings with himself have lifted him to a level of serenity that is worth struggling for. Of all the arts professors in Edinburgh he is probably the most difficult to understand, and students in a hurry have called his lectures childish. If so, it may be all the better for them. For the first half of the hour, they say, he tells you what he is going to do, and for the second half he revises. Certainly he is vastly explanatory, but then he is not so young as they are, and so he has his doubts. They are so cock-sure that they wonder to see him hesitate. Often there is a mist on the mountain when it is all clear in the valley.

Fraser's great work is his edition of Berkeley, a labour of love that should live after him. He has two Berkeleys, the large one and the little one, and, to do him justice, it was the little one he advised us to consult. I never read the large one myself, which is in a number of monster tomes, but I often had a look at it in the library, and I was proud to think that an Edinburgh professor was the editor. When Glasgow men came through to talk of their professors we showed them the big Berkeley, and after that they were reasonable.

PROFESSOR CAMPBELL FRASER

There was one man in my year who really began the large Berkeley, but after a time he was missing, and it is believed that some day he will be found flattened between the pages of the first volume.

The " Selections " was the text-book we used in the class. It is sufficient to prove that Berkeley wrote beautiful English. I am not sure that any one has written such English since. We have our own " stylists," but how self-conscious they are after Berkeley. It is seven years since I opened my " Selections," but I see that I was once more of a metaphysician than I have been giving myself credit for. The book is scribbled over with posers in my handwriting about dualism and primary realities. Some of the comments are in shorthand, which I must at one time have been able to read, but all are equally unintelligible now. Here is one of my puzzlers : — " Does B here mean impercipient and unperceived subject or conscious and percipient subject ? " Observe the friendly B. I daresay farther on I shall find myself referring to the Professor as F. I wonder if I ever discovered what B meant. I could not now tell what I meant myself.

As many persons are aware, the " Selections " consist of Berkeley's text with the Professor's notes thereon. The notes are explanatory of the text, and the student must find them an immense help. Here, for instance, is a note :—" Phenomenal or sense dependent existence can be substantiated and caused only by a self-conscious spirit, for otherwise there could be no propositions about it expressive of what is conceivable; on the other hand, to affirm that phenomenal or sense dependent existence, which alone we know, and which alone is conceivable, is, or even represents, an inconceivable non-phenomenal or abstract existence, would be to affirm a contradiction in terms." There we have it.

As a metaphysician I was something of a disappointment. I began well, standing, if I recollect aright, in the three examinations, first, seventeenth, and seventy-seventh. A man who sat beside me — man was the word we used — gazed at me reverently when I came out first, and I could see by his eye that he was not sure whether I existed properly so-called. By the second exam. his doubts had gone, and by the third he was surer of me than of himself. He came out fifty-seventh, this being the grand triumph of his college course. He was the same whose key translated *cras donaberis haedo* "To-morrow you will be presented with a kid," but who, thinking that a little vulgar, refined it down to "To-morrow you will be presented with a small child."

In the metaphysics class I was like the fountains in the quadrangle, which ran dry toward the middle of the session. While things were still looking hopeful for me, I had an invitation to breakfast with the Professor. If the fates had been so propitious as to forward me that invitation, it is possible that I might be a metaphysician to this day, but I had changed my lodgings, and when I heard of the affair, all was over. The Professor asked me to stay behind one day after the lecture, and told me that he had got his note back with "Left: no address," on it. "However," he said, "you may keep this," presenting me with the invitation for the Saturday previously. I mention this to show that even professors have hearts. That letter is preserved with the autographs of three editors, none of which anybody can read.

There was once a medical student who came up to my rooms early in the session, and I proved to him in half an hour that he did not exist. He got quite frightened, and I can still see his white face as he sat staring at me in the gloaming. This shows what metaphysics can do. He has recovered, however, and is sheep-farming now, his examiners never having asked him the right questions.

The last time Fraser ever addressed me was when I was capped. He said, "I congratulate you, Mr. Smith": and one of the other professors said, "I congratulate you, Mr. Fisher." My name is neither Smith nor Fisher, but no doubt the thing was kindly meant. It was then, however, that the professor of metaphysics had his revenge on me. I had once spelt Fraser with a "z."

VII

WHEN Chrystal came to Edinburgh he rooted up the humours of the classroom as a dentist draws teeth. Souls were sold for keys that could be carried in the waistcoat pocket. Ambition fell from heights, and lay with its eye on a certificate. By night was a rush of ghosts, shrieking for passes. Horse play fled before the Differential Calculus in spectacles.

I had Chrystal's first year, and recall the gloomy student sitting before me who hacked "All hope abandon ye who enter here" into a desk that may have confined Carlyle. It took him a session, and he was digging his own grave, for he never got through; but it was something to hold by, something he felt sure of. All else was spiders' webs in chalk.

Chrystal was a fine hare for the hounds who could keep up with him. He started off the first day with such a spurt that most of us were left behind mopping our faces, and saying, " Here's a fellow," which is what Mr. Stevenson says Shakespeare would have remarked about Mr. George Meredith. We never saw him again. The men who were on speaking acquaintance with his symbols revelled in him as students love an enthusiast who is eager to lead them into a world toward which they would journey. He was a rare guide for them. The bulk, however, lost him in labyrinths. They could not but admire their brilliant professor; but while their friend the medalist and he kept the conversation to themselves, they felt like eavesdroppers hearkening to a pair of lovers. "It is beautiful," they cried, "but this is no place for us; let us away."

A good many went, but their truancy stuck in their throats like Otway's last roll. The M. A. was before them. They had fancied it in their hands, but it became shy as a maiden from the day they learned Chrystal's heresy that Euclid is not mathematics but only some riders in it. This snapped the cord that had tied the blind man to his dog, and the M. A. shot down the horizon. When Rutherford delivered his first lecture in the chair of Institutes of Medicine, boisterous students drowned his voice, and he flung out of the room. At the door he paused to say, "Gentlemen, we shall meet again at Philippi." A dire bomb was this in the midst of them, warranted to go off, none able to cast it overboard. We, too, had our

Philippi before us. Chrystal could not be left to his own devices.

I had never a passion for knowing that when circles or triangles attempt impossibilities it is absurd; and x was an unknown quantity I was ever content to walk round about. To admit to Chrystal that we understood x was only a way he had of leading you on to y and z. I gave him his chance, however, by contributing a paper of answers to his first weekly set of exercises. When the hour for returning the slips came round, I was there to accept fame — if so it was to be — with modesty; and if it was to be humiliation, still to smile. The Professor said there was one paper, with an owner's name on it, which he could not read, and it was handed along the class to be deciphered. My presentiment that it was mine became a certainty when it reached my hand; but I passed it on pleasantly, and it returned to Chrystal, a Japhet that never found its father. Feeling that the powers were against me, I then retired from the conflict, sanguine that the teaching of my mathematical schoolmaster, the best that could be, would pull me through. The Disowned may be going the round of the classroom still.

The men who did not know when they were beaten returned to their seats, and doggedly took notes, their faces lengthening daily. Their notebooks reproduced exactly the hieroglyphics of the blackboard, and, examined at night, were as suggestive as the photographs of persons one has never seen. To overtake Chrystal after giving him a start was the presumption that is an offshoot from despair. There was once an elderly gentleman who for years read the *Times* every day from the first page to the last. For a fortnight he was ill of a fever; but, on recovering, he began at the copy of the *Times* where he had left off. He struggled magnificently to make up on the *Times*, but it was in vain. This is an allegory for the way these students panted after Chrystal.

Some succumbed and joined the majority — literally; for to mathematics they were dead. I never hear of the old University now, nor pass under the shadow of the walls one loves when he is done with them, without seeing myself as I was the day I matriculated, an awestruck boy, passing and repassing the gates, frightened to venture inside, breathing heavily at sight of janitors, Scott and Carlyle in the air. After that I see nothing fuller of colour than the meetings that were held outside Chrystal's door. Adjoining it is a classroom so little sought for, that legend tells of its door once showing the notice : " There will be no class to-day as the student is unwell." The crowd round Chrystal's could have filled that room. It was composed of students hearkening at the door to see whether he was to call their part of the roll

to-day.   If he did, they slunk in ; if not, the crowd
melted into the streets, this refrain in their ears —

> " I'm plucked, I do admit,
>   I'm spun, my mother dear,
>   Yet do not grieve for that
>   Which happens every year.
> I've waited very patiently,
>   I may have long to wait,
> But you've another son, mother,
>   And he will graduate."

A professor of mathematics once brought a
rowdy student from the back benches to a seat
beside him, because — " First, you'll be near the
board; second, you'll be near me ; and, third, you'll
be near the door."   Chrystal soon discovered that
students could be too near the door, and he took
to calling the roll in the middle of the hour, which
insured an increased attendance.   It was a silent
class, nothing heard but the patter of pencils, rats
scraping for grain, of which there was abundance,
but not one digestion in a bench.   To smuggle in
a novel up one's waistcoat was perilous, Chrystal's
spectacles doing their work.   At a corner of the
platform sat the assistant, with a constable's author-
ity, but not formed for swooping, uneasy because
he had legs, and where to put them he knew not.
He got through the hour by shifting his position
every five minutes; and, sitting there waiting, he

reminded one of the boy who, on being told to remain so quietly where he was that he could hear a pin drop, held his breath a moment, then shouted, "Let it drop!" An excellent fellow was this assistant, who told us that one of his predecessors had got three months.

A jest went as far in that class as a plum in the midshipmen's pudding, and, you remember, when the middies came on a plum they gave three cheers. In the middle of some brilliant reasoning Chrystal would stop to add 4, 7, and 11. Addition of this kind was the only thing he could not do, and he looked to the class for help — "20," they shouted, "24," "17," while he thought it over. These appeals to their intelligence made them beam. They woke up as a sleepy congregation shakes itself into life when the minister says, "I remember when I was a little boy. . . ."

The daring spirits — say, those who were going into their father's office, and so did not look upon Chrystal as a door locked to their advancement — sought to bring sunshine into the room. Chrystal soon had the blind down on that. I hear they have been at it recently with the usual result. To relieve the monotony, a student at the end of bench ten dropped a marble, which toppled slowly downward toward the Professor. At every step it took there was a smothered guffaw; but Chrystal, who was working at the board, did not turn his head. When the marble reached the floor, he said, still with his back to the class, " Will the student at the end of bench ten, who dropped that marble, stand up ? " All eyes dilated. He had counted the falls of the marble from step to step. Mathematics do not obscure the intellect.

Twenty per cent. was a good percentage in Chrystal's examinations; thirty sent you away whistling. As the M. A. drew nigh, students on their prospects might have been farmers discussing the weather. Some put their faith in the Professor's goodness of heart, of which symptoms had been showing. He would not, all at once, " raise the standard " — hated phrase until you are through, when you write to the papers advocating it. Courage! was it not told of the Glasgow Snell competition that one of the competitors, as soon as he saw the first paper, looked for his hat and the door, that he was forbidden to withdraw until an hour had elapsed, and that he then tackled the paper and ultimately carried off the Snell ? Of more immediate interest, perhaps, was the story of the quaking student, whose neighbour handed him in pencil, beneath the desk, the answer to several questions. It was in an M. A. exam., and the affrighted student found that he could not read his neighbour's notes. Trusting to fortune, he enclosed them with his own answers, writing at the top, "No time to write these out in ink, so enclose them in pencil." He got through: no moral.

A condemned criminal wondering if he is to get a reprieve will not feel the position novel, if he has loitered in a University quadrangle waiting for the janitor to nail up the results of a degree exam. A queer gathering we were, awaiting the verdict of Chrystal. Some compressed their lips, others were lively as fireworks dipped in water; there were those who rushed round and round the quadrangle; only one went the length of saying that he did not want to pass. H. I shall call him. I met him the other day in Fleet Street, and he annoyed me by asking me at once if I remembered the landlady I quarrelled with because she wore my socks to church of a Sunday: we found her out one wet forenoon. H. waited the issue with a cigar in his mouth. He had purposely, he explained, given in a bad paper. He could not understand why men were so anxious to get through. He had ten reasons for wishing to be plucked. We let him talk. The janitor appeared with the fateful paper, and we lashed about him like waves round a lighthouse, all but H., who strolled languidly to the board to which the paper was being fastened. A moment afterwards I heard a shriek, "I'm through! I'm through!" It was H. His cigar was dashed aside, and he sped like an arrow from the bow to the nearest telegraph office, shouting " I'm through! " as he ran.

Those of us who had H.'s fortune now consider Chrystal made to order for his chair, but he has never, perhaps, had a proper appreciation of the charming fellows who get ten per cent.

VIII

When one of the distinguished hunting ladies who chase celebrities captured Mr. Mark Pattison, he gave anxious consideration to the quotation which he was asked to write above his name. "Fancy," he said with a shudder, "going down to posterity arm in arm with *carpe diem!*" Remembering this, I forbear tying Sellar to *odi profanum vulgus.* Yet the name opens the door to the quotation.

Sellar is a Roman senator. He stood very high at Oxford, and took a prize for boxing. If you watch him in the class, you will sometimes see his mind murmuring that Edinburgh students do not take their play like Oxford men. The difference is in manner. A courteous fellow-student of Sellar once showed his relatives over Balliol. "You have now, I think," he said at last, "seen everything of interest except the Master." He flung a stone at a window, at which the Master's head appeared immediately, menacing, wrathful. "And now," concluded the polite youth, "you have seen him also."

233

Mr. James Payn, who never forgave the Scottish people for pulling down their blinds on Sundays, was annoyed by the halo they have woven around the name " Professor." He knew an Edinburgh lady who was scandalized because that mere poet, Alexander Smith, coolly addressed professors by their surnames. Mr. Payn might have known what it is to walk in the shadow of a Senatus Academicus, could he have met such specimens as Sellar, Fraser, Tait, and Sir Alexander Grant marching down the Bridges abreast. I have seen them: an inspiriting sight. The pavement only held three. You could have shaken hands with them from an upper window.

Sellar's treatment of his students was always that of a fine gentleman. Few got near him; all respected him. At times he was addressed in an unknown tongue, but he kept his countenance. He was particular about students keeping to their proper benches, and once thought he had caught a swarthy north countryman straying. " You are in your wrong seat, Mr. Orr." " Na, am richt eneuch." " You should be in the seat in front. That is bench 12, and you are entered on bench 10." " Eh? This is no bench twal, (counting) twa, fower, sax, aucht, ten." " There is something wrong." " Oh-h-h (with sudden enlightenment) ye've been coontin' the first dask; we dinna coont the first dask." The Professor knew the men he had to deal with too well to scorn this one, who turned out to be a fine fellow. He was the only man I ever knew who ran his medical and arts classes together, and so many lectures had he to attend daily that he mixed them up. He graduated, however, in both faculties in five years, and the last I heard of him was that, when applying for a medical assistantship, he sent his father's photograph because he did not have one of himself. He was a man of brains as well as sinew, and dined briskly on a shilling a week.

There was a little fellow in the class who was a puzzle to Sellar, because he was higher sitting than standing: when the Professor asked him to stand up, he stood down. "Is Mr. Blank not present?" Sellar would ask. "Here, sir," cried Blank. "Then, will you stand up, Mr. Blank?" (Agony of Blank, and a demonstration of many feet.) "Are you not prepared, Mr. Blank?" "Yes, sir; *Pastor quum traheret* —" "I insist on your standing up, Mr. Blank." (Several students rise to their feet to explain, but subside.) "Yes, sir; *Pastor quum traheret per* —" "I shall mark you 'not prepared,' Mr. Blank." (Further demonstration, and then an indignant squeak from Blank.) "If you please, sir, I am standing." "But, in that case, how is it —? Ah, oh, ah, yes; proceed, Mr. Blank." As one man was only called upon for exhibition five or six times in a year, the

Professor had always forgotten the circumstances when he asked Blank to stand up again. Blank was looked upon by his fellow-students as a practical jest, and his name was always received with the prolonged applause which greets the end of an after-dinner speech.

Sellar never showed resentment to the students who addressed him as Professor Sellars.

One day the Professor was giving out some English to be translated into Latin prose. He read on — " and fiercely lifting the axe with both hands —" when a cheer from the top bench made him pause. The cheer spread over the room like an uncorked gas. Sellar frowned, but proceeded — " lifting the axe —," when again the class became demented. " What does this mean ? " he demanded, looking as if he, too, could lift the axe. " Axe ! " shouted a student in explanation. Still Sellar could not solve the riddle. Another student rose to his assistance. " Axe — Gladstone ! " he cried. Sellar sat back in his chair. " Really, gentlemen," he said, " I take the most elaborate precautions against touching upon politics in this class, but sometimes you are beyond me. Let us continue — 'and fiercely lifting his weapon with both hands —.' "

The duxes from the schools suffered a little during their first year, from a feeling that they and Sellar understood each other. He liked to undeceive them. We had one, all head, who went about wondering at himself. He lost his bursary on the way home with it, and still he strutted. Sellar asked if we saw anything peculiar in a certain line from Horace. We did not. We were accustomed to trust to Horace's reputation, all but the dandy. "Eh — ah! Professor," he lisped; "it ought to have been so and so." Sellar looked at this promising plant from the schools, and watered him without a rose on the pan. "Depend upon it, Mr.—; ah, I did not catch your name, if it ought to have been so and so, Horace would have made it so and so."

Sellar's face was proof against sudden wit. It did not relax till he gave it liberty. You could never tell from it what was going on inside. He read without a twitch a notice on his door: "Found in this class a gold-headed pencil case; if not claimed within three days will be sold to defray expenses." He even withstood the battering ram on the day of the publication of his "Augustan Poets." The students could not let this opportunity pass. They assailed him with frantic applause — every bench was a drum to thump upon. His countenance said nothing. The drums had it in the end, though, and he dismissed the class with what is believed to have verged on a smile. Like the lover who has got his lady's glance, they at once tried for more, but no.

Most of us had Humanity our first year, which is the year for experimenting. Then is the time to join the University library. The pound, which makes you a member, has never had its poet. You can withdraw your pound when you please. There are far-seeing men who work the whole thing out by mathematics. Put simply, this is the notion. In the beginning of the session you join the library, and soon you forget about your pound; you reckon without it. As the winter closes in, and the coal-bunk empties; or you find that five shillings a week for lodgings is a dream that cannot be kept up; or your coat assumes more and more the colour identified with spring; or you would feast your friends for once right gloriously; or next Wednesday is your little sister's birthday; you cower, despairing, over a sulky fire. Suddenly you are on your feet, all aglow once more. What is this thought that sends the blood to your head? That library pound! You had forgotten that you had a bank. Next morning you are at the university in time to help the library door to open. You ask for your pound; you get it. Your hand mounts guard over the pocket in which it rustles. So they say. I took their advice and paid in my money; then waited exultingly to forget about it. In vain. I always allowed for that pound in my thoughts. I saw it as plainly, I knew its every feature as a schoolboy remembers his first trout. Not to be hasty, I gave my pound two months, and then brought it home again. I had a fellow-student who lived across the way from me. We railed at the library pound theory at open windows over the life of the street; a beautiful dream, but mad, mad.

He was an enthusiast, and therefore happy, whom I have seen in the Humanity classroom on an examination day, his pen racing with time, himself seated in the contents of an ink-bottle. Some stories of exams. have even a blacker ending. I write in tears of him who, estimating his memory as a leaky vessel, did with care and forethought draw up a crib that was more condensed than a pocket cyclopædia, a very Liebig's essence of the classics, tinned meat for students in the eleventh hour. Bridegrooms have been known to forget the ring; this student forgot his crib. In the middle of the examination came a nervous knocking at the door. A lady wanted to see the Professor at once. The student looked up, to see his mother handing the Professor his crib. Her son had forgotten it; she was sure that it was important, so she had brought it herself.

Jump the body of this poor victim. There was no M. A. for him that year; but in our gowns and sashes we could not mourn for a might-have-been. Soldiers talk of the Victoria Cross, statesmen of the Cabinet, ladies of a pearl set in diamonds. These are pretty baubles, but who has thrilled as the student that with bumping heart strolls into Middlemass's to order his graduate's gown. He hires it — five shillings — but the photograph to follow makes it as good as his for life. Look at him, young ladies, as he struts to the Synod Hall to have M. A. tacked to his name. Dogs do not dare bark at him. His gait is springy; in Princes Street he is as one who walks upstairs. Gone to me are those student days for ever, but I can still put a photograph before me of a ghost in gown and cape, the hair straggling under the cap as tobacco may straggle over the side of a tin when there is difficulty in squeezing down the lid. How well the little black jacket looks, how vividly the wearer remembers putting it on. He should have worn a dress-coat, but he had none. The little jacket resembled one with the tails off, and, as he artfully donned his gown, he backed against the wall so that no one might know.

To turn up the light on old college days is not always the signal for the dance. You are back in the dusty little lodging, with its battered sofa, its slippery tablecloth, the prim array of books, the picture of the death of Nelson, the peeling walls, the broken clock; you are again in the quadrangle with him who has been dead this many a year. There are tragedies in a college course.

Dr. Walter Smith has told in a poem mentioned elsewhere of the brilliant scholar who forgot his dominie; some, alas! forget their mother. There are men — I know it — who go mad from loneliness; and medalists ere now have crept home to die. The capping-day was the end of our springtide, and for some of us the summer was to be brief. Sir Alexander, gone into the night since then, flung " I mekemae " at us as we trooped past him, all in bud, some small flower to blossom in time, let us hope, here and there.

IX

Two years hence Joseph Thomson's reputation will be a decade old, though he is at present only thirty years of age. When you meet him for the first time you conclude that he must be the explorer's son. His identity, however, can always be proved by simply mentioning Africa in his presence. Then he draws himself up, and his eyes glisten, and he is thinking how glorious it would be to be in the Masai country again, living on meat so diseased that it crumbled in the hand like short-bread.

Gatelaw-bridge Quarry, in Dumfriesshire, is famous for Old Mortality and Thomson, the latter (when he is at the head of a caravan) being as hardheaded as if he had been cut out of it. He went to school at Thornhill, where he spent great part of his time in reading novels, and then he matriculated at Edinburgh University, where he began to accumulate medals. Geology and kindred studies were his favourites there. One day he heard that Keith Johnston, then on the point

242

of starting for Africa, wanted a lieutenant. Thomson son was at that time equally in need of a Keith Johnston, and everybody who knew him saw that the opening and he were made for each other. Keith Johnston and Thomson went out together, and Johnston died in the jungle. This made a man in an hour of a stripling. Most youths in Thomson's position at that turning point of his career would have thought it judicious to turn back, and in geographical circles it would have been considered highly creditable had he brought his caravan to the coast intact. Thomson, however, pushed on, and did everything that his dead leader had hoped to do. From that time his career has been followed by every one interested in African exploration, and by his countrymen with some pride in addition. When an expedition was organized for the relief of Emin Pasha, there was for a time some probability of Thomson's having the command. He and Stanley differed as to the routes that should be taken, and subsequent events have proved that Thomson's was the proper one.

Thomson came over from Paris at that time to consult with the authorities, and took up his residence in the most over-grown hotel in London. His friends here organized an expedition for his relief. They wandered up and down the endless stairs looking for him, till, had they not wanted to make themselves a name, they would have beaten a retreat. He also wandered about looking for them, and at last they met. The leader of the party, restraining his emotion, lifted his hat, and said, " Mr. Thomson, I presume ? " This is how I found Thomson.

The explorer had been for some months in Paris at that time, and France did him the honour of translating his " Through Masailand " into French. In this book there is a picture of a buffalo tossing Thomson in the air. This was after he had put several bullets into it, and in the sketch he is represented some ten feet from the ground, with his gun flying one way and his cap another. " It was just as if I were distributing largess to the natives," the traveller says now, though this idea does not seem to have struck him at the time. He showed the sketch to a Parisian lady, who looked at it long and earnestly. " Ah, M. Thomson," she said at length, " but how could you pose like that ? "

Like a good many other travellers, including Mr. Du Chaillu, who says he is a dear boy, Thomson does not smoke. Stanley, however, smokes very strong cigars, as those who have been in his sumptuous chambers in Bond Street can testify. All the three happen to be bachelors, though ; because, one of them says, after returning from years of lonely travel, a man has such a delight in female society that to pick and choose would be invidious.

Yet they have had their chance. An African race once tried to bribe Mr. Du Chaillu with a kingdom and over eight hundred wives,— "the biggest offer," he admits, "I ever had in one day."

Among the lesser annoyances to which Thomson was subjected in Africa was the presence of rats in the night-time, which he had to brush away like flies. Until he was asked whether there was not danger in this, it never seems to have struck him that it was more than annoying. Yet though he and the two other travellers mentioned (doubtless they are not alone in this) have put up cheerfully with almost every hardship known to man, this does not make them indifferent to the comforts of civilization when they return home. Du-Chaillu was looking very comfortable in a house-boat the other day, where his hosts thought they were "roughing it"— with a male attendant; and in Stanley's easy chairs you sink to dream. The last time I saw Thomson in his rooms in London he was on his knees, gazing in silent rapture at a china saucer with a valuable crack in it.

If you ask Thomson what was the most dangerous expedition he ever embarked on, he will probably reply, "Crossing Piccadilly." The finest thing that can be said of him is that during these four expeditions he never once fired a shot at a native. Other explorers have had to do so to save their lives. There were often occasions when

Thomson could have done it, to save his life to all appearance, too. The result of his method of progressing is that where he has gone — and he has been in parts of Africa never before trod by the white man — he really has " opened up the country " for those who care to follow him. Civilization by bullet has only closed it elsewhere. Yet though there is an abundance of Scotch caution about him, he is naturally an impulsive man, more inclined personally to march straight on than to reach his destination by a safer if more circuitous route. Where only his own life is concerned he gives you the impression of one who might be rash, but his prudence at the head of a caravan is at the bottom of the faith that is placed in him. According to a story that got into the papers years ago, M. de Brazza once quarrelled with Thomson in Africa, and all but struck him. Thomson was praised for keeping his temper. The story was a fabrication, but I fear that if M. de Brazza had behaved like this, Thomson would not have remembered to be diplomatic till some time afterwards. A truer tale might be told of an umbrella, gorgeous and wonderful to behold, that De Brazza took to Africa to impress the natives with, and which Thomson subsequently presented to a dusky monarch.

The explorer has never shot a lion, though he has tracked a good many of them. Once he thought he had one. It was reclining in a little grove, and Thomson felt that it was his at last. With a trusty native he crept forward till he could obtain a good shot, and then fired. In breathless suspense he waited for its spring, and then when it did not spring he saw that he had shot it through the heart. However, it turned out only to be a large stone.

The young Scotchman sometimes thinks of the tremendous effect it would have had on the natives had he been the possessor of a complete set of artificial teeth. This is because he has one artificial tooth. Happening to take it out one day, an awe filled all who saw him, and from that hour he was esteemed a medicine man. Another excellent way of impressing Africa with the grandeur of Britain was to take a photograph. When the natives saw the camera aimed at them they fell to the ground vanquished.

When Thomson was recently in this country, he occasionally took a walk of twenty or thirty miles to give him an appetite for dinner. This he calls a stroll. One day he strolled from Thornhill to Edinburgh, had dinner, and then went to the Exhibition. In appearance he is tall and strongly knit rather than heavily built, and if you see him more than once in the same week, you discover that he has still an interest in neckties. Perhaps his most remarkable feat consisted in taking a bottle of brandy into the heart of Africa, and bringing it back intact.

X

ROBERT LOUIS STEVENSON

Some men of letters, not necessarily the greatest, have an indescribable charm to which we give our hearts. Thackeray is the young man's first love. Of living authors none perhaps bewitches the reader more than Mr. Stevenson, who plays upon words as if they were a musical instrument. To follow the music is less difficult than to place the musician. A friend of mine, who, like Mr. Grant Allen, reviews 365 books a year, and 366 in leap years, recently arranged the novelists of to-day in order of merit. Meredith, of course, he wrote first, and then there was a fall to Hardy. "Haggard," he explained, "I dropped from the Eiffel Tower; but what can I do with Stevenson? I can't put him before 'Lorna Doone.'" So Mr. Stevenson puzzles the critics, fascinating them until they are willing to judge him by the great work he is to write by and by when the little books are finished. Over "Treasure Island" I let my fire die in winter without knowing that I was freezing. But the creator of Alan Breck has now published nearly twenty volumes. It is so much easier to finish the little works than to begin the great one, for which we are all taking notes.

Mr. Stevenson is not to be labelled novelist. He wanders the byways of literature without any fixed address. Too much of a truant to be classified with the other boys, he is only a writer of fiction in the sense that he was once an Edinburgh University student because now and again he looked in at his classes when he happened to be that way. A literary man without a fixed occupation amazes Mr. Henry James, a master in the school of fiction which tells, in three volumes, how Hiram K. Wilding trod on the skirt of Alice M. Sparkins without anything's coming of it. Mr. James analyzes Mr. Stevenson with immense cleverness, but without summing up. That " Dr. Jekyll and Mr. Hyde " should be by the author of " Treasure Island," " Virginibus Puerisque " by the author of " The New Arabian Nights," " A Child's Garden of Verses " by the author of " Prince Otto," are to him the three degrees of comparison of wonder, though for my own part I marvel more that the author of " Daisy Miller " should be Mr. Stevenson's eulogist. One conceives Mr. James a boy in velveteens looking fearfully at Stevenson playing at pirates.

There is nothing in Mr. Stevenson's sometimes writing essays, sometimes romances. and anon poems to mark him versatile beyond other authors. One dreads his continuing to do so, with so many books at his back, lest it means weakness rather than strength. He experiments too long; he is still a boy wondering what he is going to be. With Cowley's candour he tells us that he wants to write something by which he may be for ever known. His attempts in this direction have been in the nature of trying different ways, and he always starts off whistling. Having gone so far without losing himself, he turns back to try another road. Does his heart fail him, despite his jaunty bearing, or is it because there is no hurry? Though all his books are obviously by the same hand, no living writer has come so near fame from so many different sides. Where is the man among us who could write another "Virginibus Puerisque," the most delightful volume for the hammock ever sung in prose? The poems are as exquisite as they are artificial. "Jekyll and Hyde" is the greatest triumph extant in Christmas literature of the morbid kind. The donkey on the Cevennes (how Mr. Stevenson belaboured him!) only stands second to the "Inland Voyage." "Kidnapped" is the outstanding boy's book of its generation. "The Black Arrow" alone, to my thinking, is second-class. We shall all be doleful if a marksman who can pepper his target with inners does not reach the bull's-eye. But it is quite time the great work was begun. The sun sinks while the climber walks round his mountain, looking for the best way up.

Hard necessity has kept some great writers from doing their best work, but Mr. Stevenson is at last so firmly established that if he continues to be versatile it will only be from choice. He has attained a popularity such as is, as a rule, only accorded to classic authors or to charlatans. For this he has America to thank rather than Britain, for the Americans buy his books, the only honour a writer's admirers are slow to pay him. Mr. Stevenson's reputation in the United States is creditable to that country, which has given him a position here in which only a few saw him when he left. Unfortunately, with popularity has come publicity. All day the reporters sit on his garden wall.

No man has written in a finer spirit of the profession of letters than Mr. Stevenson, but this gossip vulgarizes it. The adulation of the American public and of a little band of clever literary dandies in London, great in criticism, of whom he has become the darling, has made Mr. Stevenson complacent, and he always tended perhaps to be a thought too fond of his velvet coat. There is danger in the delight with which his every scrap is now received. A few years ago, when he was his own severest and sanest critic, he stopped the pub-

lication of a book after it was in proof — a brave
act. He has lost this courage, or he would have
re-written " The Black Arrow." There is dete-
rioration in the essays he has been contributing to
an American magazine, graceful and suggestive
though they are. The most charming of living
stylists, Mr. Stevenson is self-conscious in all his
books now and again, but hitherto it has been the
self-consciousness of an artist with severe critics at
his shoulder. It has become self-satisfaction. The
critics have put a giant's robe on him, and he has
not flung it off. He dismisses " Tom Jones " with
a simper. Personally Thackeray " scarce appeals
to us as the ideal gentleman; if there were nothing else [what else is there?], perpetual nosing
after snobbery at least suggests the snob." From
Mr. Stevenson one would not have expected the
revival of this silly charge, which makes a cab-
bage of every man who writes about cabbages. I
shall say no more of these ill-considered papers,
though the sneers at Fielding call for indignant
remonstrance, beyond expressing a hope that they
lie buried between magazine covers. Mr. Stevenson has reached the critical point in his career, and
one would like to see him back at Bournemouth,
writing within high walls. We want that big
book ; we think he is capable of it, and so we cannot afford to let him drift into the seaweed. About
the writer with whom his name is so often absurdly

linked we feel differently. It is as foolish to rail
at Mr. Rider Haggard's complacency as it would
be to blame Christopher Sly for so quickly believ-
ing that he was born a lord.

The key-note of all Mr. Stevenson's writings is his
indifference, so far as his books are concerned, to
the affairs of life and death on which other minds
are chiefly set. Whether man has an immortal
soul interests him as an artist not a whit: what is
to come of man troubles him as little as where
man came from. He is a warm, genial writer, yet
this is so strange as to seem inhuman. His philosophy is that we are but as the light-hearted
birds. This is our moment of being; let us play
the intoxicating game of life beautifully, artisti-
cally, before we fall dead from the tree. We all
know it is only in his books that Mr. Stevenson
can live this life. The cry is to arms; spears
glisten in the sun; see the brave bark riding joyously on the waves, the black flag, the dash of red
colour twisting round a mountainside. Alas! the
drummer lies on a couch beating his drum. It is
a pathetic picture, less true to fact now, one re-
joices to know, than it was recently. A common
theory is that Mr. Stevenson dreams an ideal life
to escape from his own sufferings. This sentimental plea suits very well. The noticeable thing,
however, is that the grotesque, the uncanny, holds
his soul; his brain will only follow a coloured

clue. The result is that he is chiefly picturesque, and, to those who want more than art for art's sake, never satisfying. Fascinating as his verses are, artless in the perfection of art, they take no reader a step forward. The children of whom he sings so sweetly are cherubs without souls. It is not in poetry that Mr. Stevenson will give the great book to the world, nor will it, I think, be in the form of essays. Of late he has done nothing quite so fine as " Virginibus Puerisque," though most of his essays are gardens in which grow few weeds. Quaint in matter as in treatment, they are the best strictly literary essays of the day, and their mixture of tenderness with humour suggests Charles Lamb. Some think Mr. Stevenson's essays equal to Lamb's, or greater. To that I say No. The name of Lamb will for many a year bring proud tears to English eyes. Here was a man, weak like the rest of us, who kept his sorrows to himself. Life to him was not among the trees. He had loved and lost. Grief laid a heavy hand on his brave brow. Dark were his nights; horrid shadows in the house; sudden terrors; the heart stops beating waiting for a footstep. At that door comes Tragedy, knocking at all hours. Was Lamb dismayed? The tragedy of his life was not drear to him. It was wound round those who were dearest to him; it let him know that life has a glory even at its saddest, that humour and pathos clasp hands, that loved ones are drawn nearer, and the soul strengthened in the presence of anguish, pain, and death. When Lamb sat down to write he did not pull down his blind on all that is greatest, if most awful, in human life. He was gentle, kindly; but he did not play at pretending that there is no cemetery round the corner. In Mr. Stevenson's exquisite essays one looks in vain for the great heart that palpitates through the pages of Charles Lamb.

The great work, if we are not to be disappointed, will be fiction. Mr. Stevenson is said to feel this himself, and, as I understand, "Harry Shovel" will be his biggest bid for fame. It is to be, broadly speaking, a nineteenth-century "Peregrine Pickle," dashed with Meredith, and this in the teeth of many admirers who maintain that the best of the author is Scottish. Mr. Stevenson, however, knows what he is about. Critics have said enthusiastically — for it is difficult to write of Mr. Stevenson without enthusiasm — that Alan Breck is as good as anything in Scott. Alan Breck is certainly a masterpiece, quite worthy of the greatest of all storytellers, who, nevertheless, it should be remembered, created these rich side characters by the score, another before dinner-time. English critics have taken Alan to their hearts, and appreciate him thoroughly; the reason, no doubt, being that he is the character whom England acknowledges as the Scottish type. The Highlands, which are Scotland to the same extent as Northumberland is England, present such a character to this day, but no deep knowledge of Mr. Stevenson's native country was required to reproduce him. An artistic Englishman or American could have done it. Scottish religion, I think, Mr. Stevenson has never understood, except as the outsider misunderstands it. He thinks it hard because there are no coloured windows. "The colour of Scotland has entered into him altogether," says Mr. James, who, we gather, conceives in Edinburgh Castle a place where tartans glisten in the sun, while rocks re-echo bagpipes. Mr. James is right in a way. It is the tartan, the claymore, the cry that the heather is on fire, that are Scotland to Mr. Stevenson. But the Scotland of our day is not a country rich in colour; a sombre grey prevails. Thus, though Mr. Stevenson's best romance is Scottish, that is only, I think, because of his extraordinary aptitude for the picturesque. Give him any period in any country that is romantic, and he will soon steep himself in the kind of knowledge he can best turn to account. Adventures suit him best, the ladies being left behind; and so long as he is in fettle it matters little whether the scene be Scotland or Spain. The

great thing is that he should now give to one am-
bitious book the time in which he has hitherto
written half a dozen small ones.   He will have to
take existence a little more seriously — to weave
broadcloth instead of lace.

XI

DURING the four winters another and I were in Edinburgh we never entered any but Free churches. This seems to have been less on account of a scorn for other denominations than because we never thought of them. We felt sorry for the " men " who knew no better than to claim to be on the side of Dr. Macgregor. Even our Free kirks were limited to two, St. George's and the Free High. After all, we must have been liberally minded beyond most of our fellows, for, as a rule, those who frequented one of these churches shook their heads at the other. It is said that Dr. Whyte and Dr. Smith have a great appreciation of each other. They, too, are liberally minded.

To contrast the two leading Free Church ministers in Edinburgh as they struck a student would be to become a boy again. The one is always ready to go on fire, and the other is sometimes at hand with a jug of cold water. Dr. Smith counts a hundred before he starts, whilst the minister of Free St. George's is off at once at a gallop, and would always arrive first at his destination if he had not sometimes to turn back. He is not only a Gladstonian, but Gladstonian; his enthusiasm carries him on as steam drives the engine. Dr. Smith being a critic, with a faculty of satire, what would rouse the one man makes the other smile. Dr. Whyte judges you as you are at the moment; Dr. Smith sees what you will be like to-morrow. Some years ago the defeated side in a great Assembly fight met at a breakfast to reason itself into a belief that it had gained a remarkable moral victory. Dr. Whyte and Dr. Smith were both present, and the former was so inspiriting that the breakfast became a scene of enthusiasm. Then Dr. Smith arose and made a remark about a company of Mark Tapleys — after which the meeting broke up.

I have a curious reminiscence of the student who most frequently accompanied me to church in Edinburgh. One Sunday when we were on our way up slushy Bath Street to Free St. George's he discovered that he had not a penny for the plate. I suggested to him to give twopence next time; but no, he turned back to our lodgings for the penny. Sometime afterwards he found himself in the same position when we were nearing the Free High. "I'll give twopence next time," he said, cheerfully. I have thought this over since then, and wondered if there was anything in it.

The most glorious privilege of the old is to assist the young.   The two ministers who are among
the chief pillars of the Free Church in Edinburgh
are not old yet, but they have had a long expe-
rience, and the strength and encouragement they
have been to the young is the grand outstanding
fact of their ministries.   Their influence is, of
course, chiefly noticeable in the divinity men, who
make their Bible classes so remarkable.   There is
a sort of Freemasonry among the men who have
come under the influence of Dr. Smith.   It seems
to have steadied them — to have given them wise
rules of life that have taken the noise out of them,
and left them undemonstrative, quiet, determined.
You will have little difficulty, as a rule, in picking
out Dr. Smith's men, whether in the pulpit or in
private.   They have his mark, as the Rugby boys
were marked by Dr. Arnold.   Even in speaking
of him, they seldom talk in superlatives: only a
light comes into their eye, and you realize what a
well-founded reverence is.   I met lately in London
an Irishman who, when the conversation turned to
Scotland, asked what Edinburgh was doing without Dr. Smith (who was in America at the time).
He talked with such obvious knowledge of Dr.
Smith's teaching, and with such affection for the
man, that by and by we were surprised to hear that
he had never heard him preach nor read a line

of his works. He explained that he knew intimately two men who looked upon their Sundays in the Free High, and still more upon their private talks with the minister, as the turning point in their lives. They were such fine fellows, and they were so sure that they owed their development to Dr. Smith, that to know the followers was to know something of the master. This it is to be a touchstone to young men.

There are those who think Dr. Smith the poet of higher account than Dr. Smith the preacher. I do not agree with them, though there can be no question that the author of " Olrig Grange " and Mr. Alexander Anderson are the two men now in Edinburgh who have (at times) the divine afflatus. " Surface-man " is a true son of Burns. Of him it may be said, as it never can be said of Dr. Smith, that he sings because he must. His thoughts run in harmonious numbers. The author of " Olrig Grange " is the stronger mind, however, and his lines are always pregnant of meaning. He is of the school of Mr. Lewis Morris, but an immeasurably higher intellect if not so fine an artist : indeed, though there are hundreds of his pages that are not poetry, there are almost none that could not be rewritten into weighty prose. Sound is never his sole object. Good novels in verse are a mistake, for it is quite certain they would be better in prose. The novelist has a great deal to say that cannot be said naturally in rhythm, and much of Dr. Smith's blank verse is good prose in frills. It is driven into an undeserved confinement.

The privilege of critics is to get twelve or twenty minor poets in a row, and then blow them all over at once. I remember one who dispatched Dr. Smith with a verse from the book under treatment. Dr. Smith writes of a poet's verses: " There is no sacred fire in them, Nor much of homely sense and shrewd," and when the critic came to these lines, he stopped reading: he declared that Dr. Smith had passed judgment on himself. This is a familiar form of criticism, but in the present case it had at least the demerit of being false. There is so much sacred fire about Dr. Smith's best poetry, that it is what makes him a poet; and as for " homely sense and shrewd," he has simply more of it than any contemporary writer of verse. It is what gives heart to his satire, and keeps him from wounding merely for the pleasure of drawing blood. In conjunction with the sacred fire, the noble indignation that mean things should be, the insight into the tragic, it is what makes " Hilda" his greatest poem. Without it there could not be pathos, which is concerned with little things; nor humour, nor, indeed, the flash into men and things that makes such a poem as " Dr. Linkletter's Scholar " as true as life, as sad as death.

REV. WALTER C. SMITH, D. D.

If only for the sake of that noble piece of writing, every Scottish student should have " North-Country Folk " in his possession. The poem is probably the most noteworthy thing that has been said of Northern University life.